Little Bird

A Why-Choose Mafia Romance

Nichole Steel

Book Cover by Covers By Sophie

Edited by Waddle Editing

First edition March 2025

Published by Nichole Steel

https://bio.site/NicholeSteel

nicholesteel.author@gmail.com

Contents

Trigger Warnings

Kidnapping

Needles

Sexual assault and rape (not on page just in FMC past)

Gun & knife violence

Torture

Drugging

Open door sex scenes with multiple males

Light BDSM

Light fat shaming (not by MMCs, just in her past)

Human trafficking

Spanking

Swearing

Character experiencing anxiety/PTSD

Double Penetration

Anal

Voyeurism

Dedication

To those who silently struggle with the demons of the past.

You are seen

You are loved.

Playlist

1. "Stop Fighting It" by April Jai

2. "Take Me Back To Eden" by Sleep Token

3. "The Monster" by Eminem, Rihanna

4. "Sweet Heart Lightning" by Gregory Alan Isakov

5. "Blood//Water" by Grandson

Chapter 1
Chelsey

"Lizzy, you're up in two songs. Hurry up or Lynal will have your ass!" Slim comes rushing into the locker room from the floor. Her glowing dark skin is sprinkled with sweat, and I can't help but roll my eyes and wave her off.

Leaning into my black hole of a locker cubby, I try like hell to convince myself the seclusion of this job is worth everything we have to deal with.

Slim scoffs and I turn as she sits at her locker while the other girls apply too much make-up and change into clothes that barely cover their most intimate of parts.

This is what we do here at Players. We get naked and allow random men to touch us all so we can survive this messed up world we live in.

I shake my head, exhausted of running on the stupid hamster wheel. Always striving to find more, but never getting anywhere.

"Lizzy! Move it girl!" Slim playfully barks at me, nudging me with her hip.

I should be moving, but sitting on the locker room bench in my comfy clothes is kind of my happy place at the moment.

Nodding, I turn back to my cubbyhole. I know I need to get ready, but the weight of dancing on the floor tonight feels extra heavy.

I want to be one of those girls from the movies where the guy showers her with all the love and tenderness, where she's worth more than what her body can do. I want a life where I have choices and freedom to be who I want to be. To maybe even find a happily ever after, but that is just stupid fantasy shit. The reality is that women are here to serve men, nothing more.

A woman is only as good as her pussy. That's what dad always told me anyways.

Blowing out a breath, I stand, removing my comfy sweats and panties, then slide on the thin pink thong. Next goes my warm sweatshirt for a black fishnet mesh bra. They don't cover much, but it's better than walking out on the floor naked.

"Time to face the fucking music I guess..." I mutter to Slim, who is oiling her body to give it a nice shine under the lights. I'm not that committed.

"Kick ass on the pole, girl." She winks at me as I shove the last of my stuff into my cubbyhole.

"You know I always do." I toss my hair over my shoulder and turn to stick my tongue out at her as I leave the sanctuary of the back room.

The floor is flooded with people tonight and the neon lights make the two girls on stage look like goddesses. There's no way they won't be taking men to the lounge rooms after their dances.

The lounge VIP dances are where the money is, but it's also where you have to rub your mostly naked body all over the horny bastards. Letting men that are pigs touch me is nothing new, but at least here I get paid for it.

Most nights I try my best to be thankful for this job. It pays cash, allowing me to go unnoticed by society and be pretty much completely hidden. This job is my sanctuary, and I try like hell to remember that, because I want to quit every single day.

My song is on next, and I begrudgingly climb the stage. The music fills the room, and I take hold of the pole, grinding on it to the pulsing thrum of the beat. The men gather around the stage, throwing dollars towards me.

The more they pay me, the more I do.

It's a game to engage the men; they like seeing what their dollars can get them. I let my large boobs spring free, and some asshole has the actual nerve to whistle at me.

I rake my eyes over the men seductively, and most are regulars. But I spot a new man in the corner and lock my gaze on him as I dance.

His sea-blue eyes glow under the lights, holding me captive till I dip and take the rest of him in. Burly looking, with shaggy black hair, and earring studs in each lobe. His facial hair is thick and groomed, looking almost manicured over his firm, sculpted face.

The suit straining tight against his sculpted arms looks to be worth a thousand dollars alone. He is definitely the most well-dressed person here and men like that throw more than a dollar or two on the stage at a time. I have a feeling a dance with this guy could cover my rent for a month. Biting my lip, I leave the pole, crawling across the stage towards him, never breaking eye contact. Men like a submissive woman.

Crawl to me princess... I will away the monster's voice in my head, the man who taught me what men like.

Running my tongue over my upper lip, I start bouncing on my knees, fondling my tits, almost like I am bouncing on a cock. *Come on honey, come throw your money at me.*

If I can hook this guy, he might come back. I would love him as a regular.

Please baby, you know you want this. I'm basically begging him with my body at this point, but he doesn't move.

Someone to my left tucks money into my thong strap, so I turn and start twerking in his face, bouncing my pelvis off the floor to give my ass more jiggle. The man smacks my ass with a sharp sting, but I ignore it. He tucks more money to my thong strap and I turn to face him.

"Want some titties?" I splay my chest out to him.

"Hell yeah." I grab his shoulders and pull him to me as I rub my boobs in his face. *Please let this song be almost over...*

His hand holds cash as he rubs it down my rib cage, tucking it into the front of my thong, dangerously close to the apex of my thighs. Anxiety fills my gut, and I move back so he can no long touch, but only look. I swear if you give these guys an inch they try for a mile.

My song finally ends, and I quickly move to grab my cash and climb off the stage so the next girl can take my place.

The new guy doesn't move from his seat, only takes a sip from a whiskey glass at his table, but his eyes never leave me.

Prickles run over my skin as heat rushes between my thighs. There is something about this man that is both terrifying and alluring.

One of the regulars who seems to always love my company starts moving my way. The old man rarely showers and always smells like booze. He's a gross creep and I would rather give a dance to anyone else in this place, but money is money at this point. If I don't take the VIP dances I can't eat.

The new guy leaves his seat and *fuck* is he massive, easily six foot five, and is moving towards me just like the old man. Guess he was intrigued after all. Not that anyone could tell by the stoic look on his face.

"It seems you got plenty of a show on the stage." New guy's eyes bore into mine. "My turn now. I already paid for an All-Star with her." The new guy sneers to the other guy, finally breaking our gaze. Almost like he's marking his territory.

His voice is deep and smooth, making things light up in all the right places, but I cannot go there.

And I can't let the guys see every fiber of me is screaming in suppressed rage. I'm the plaything for hire right now and if

7

I want to keep my job, I need to keep that image, and I need this job...

"Well I look forward to your company, sugar, but I need to speak with my manager before we head on back." I offer a seductive smile and march towards Lynal in the booth, smoke damn near rolling out of my ears.

"What the fuck Lynal?" I hiss at him. "I may strip for you, but I'm not one of your whores." I keep my voice low, but I'm fuming. All-Stars are more than just teasing. They are full on sex and Lynal knows I don't do them. I have been told who to fuck most of my adult life, and I refuse to do that anymore.

"Hey, he came in here, asked for you by name, and paid two-thousand to fuck you. You're going to make fifteen-hundred tonight, so go get your man, use your pussy, and be thankful for the blessing," Lynal barks at me and I jump a little at his tone.

"Fuck you, Lynal!" I say, seething towards him.

Fuck it, it's not worth the fight tonight. Really it shouldn't bother me. It's not like I'm not used to being passed around. I just wish I wasn't.

My father has had me servicing his Northside Gang since I was eighteen.

Shaking away my frustration, I stand straight and put a smile on my face.

I will fuck this pig of a man tonight, take my money, and find a new job, because I'll starve before Lynal turns me into another one of his whores.

Making my way back to the man who bought my company, I put on the mask I have worn for years. *'I enjoy this and can't wait to be in your presence.'*

"Alright sugar, right this way." I smile at him and grab his tie, leading him to the far back lounge room that is strictly used for All-Star treatments. It has locks, soundproofing, and a bed. My gentleman doesn't balk, just wears a crooked smile.

I mean if I have to fuck someone, there are worse looking guys out there. And I would be lying if I said I wasn't a little curious to see him without a shirt. I mean his shirt is straining against his arms and shoulders so much that if he flexed, it may actually rip!

Once in the room, I release him and turn to face the door, locking it behind us. *You have been fucking guys like this forever.*

Get it done and you're set for a month. I let out a breath. No matter how many times I have sex with someone I don't want to, it never seems to get any easier.

Turning to face him, I have to hide my surprise. He's sitting on the edge of the bed, fully dressed, with his ankles crossed. *Apparently he likes foreplay.* Most would be half naked before the door is even locked.

I saunter over to him with a seductive sway in my hips. I know the act well.

"Sweetheart, you can stop right there," he commands with a dark voice, as smooth as the finest of whiskeys.

Well this is new. A man who pays for my company doesn't stop me before I've even touched him.

"I don't need you to fuck me Chelsey, I just needed those other men to stop touching you." His voice is deep and firm.

Fuck. Panic rises in my chest, sweat coating my palms, but I don't move from my spot.

How did they find me? I was careful, so incredibly careful!

"How do you know my real name?" I say with an edge to my tone.

"Oh, I know everything there is to know about you," he coos at me with a cocky smile. "I know you're twenty-two. That you're staying at a run-down trailer two blocks from here. And that you ran away from your father because he was going to sell you as a concubine to the leader of the Chicago Italian Mafia." He pushes off the bed and backs me up to the door, grabbing my chin. "You have not been easy to find. Though my brothers and I do love a good challenge." He leans closer to me and I shutter at his proximity. "But you were extra difficult to track down," he growls.

No one knew of my father's plans to sell me. The only reason I knew is because I overheard him talking to my step-mother.

How else is she going to earn her keep? I have our sons to carry on the family line, so she will do what a woman was made to do. She will go to Riccardo, be fucked to his heart's desire and strengthen the ties between our gang and the Italian Mafia.

I struggle, trying to break free from the man holding me, but we both know I don't have a chance of getting away.

"Well since you know all about me. Why don't you tell me who you are?" I bat my eyes at him.

Men are all the same, they all want a good lay. If I can get him into bed, I might have a chance at hitting him with the lamp on the nightstand, buying me enough time to get the hell out of here.

Lacing my fingers into his shirt, I press my pelvis into him.

"My brothers and I are the head of the Romano Crime Family." He grabs my hands, pinning them above my head with a condescending smirk. "When we heard what Riccardo was willing to pay for you, we decided to start tracking you ourselves. We were pretty happy when we found you here... In our own territory." He coos at me, running a thumb down my cheek and I turn away. *Fucking bastard...*

Adrenaline floods my system, but I cannot let the panic win. Taking a deep breath, I slow my heart and face him head on, hoping he can't see the emotion underneath my glare.

"So, your plan is to sell me to Riccardo then? Send me back to Chicago?" I scoff at him. Yet under all the bravado, I'm terrified of returning.

"Oh no, you misunderstand. If Riccardo wants you, you must be a hell of a prize," he jeers, leaning close to my ear. "No, we intend to keep you for ourselves."

Relief surges through me. *This could be worse.* I can buy time with them and then escape again.

"Well if I'm going to stay with you, what's your name, sugar?" I coo at him and bat my lashes, sliding my leg between his.

"I am Nico, but you may call me Nic." He releases me from the door, and I drive my knee up hard and shove his chest hard.

He effectively blocks my knee, only stumbling back a step or two.

I turn and scramble for the lock, but before I can twist the knob, I'm pressed flat to the door.

I let out a soft whimper of pain, my chest screaming from the harsh pressure.

He is firm and unyielding in his hold as I fight against him, tears threatening my eyes. There is no escape. That was my one chance...

"I'll give you props for trying." His voice is a deep growl, and I can feel his chest vibrate as he speaks. He takes hold of my throat and spins me to face him. My stomach jumps to my throat at the look of pure rage in his eyes. "But if you ever do that again, I'll kill you where you stand." All the air in my lungs leave and he leans close enough that our noses almost touch. "Do you understand me?"

I'm frozen, my mind trying to sort out what to do next.

"Do. You. Understand. Me." He raises his voice with each clipped word and I drop my gaze.

There is nothing left to do but submit to my new captor.

"Yes," I mutter, and the word sounds so damn weak.

"Yes what?" he sneers.

"Yes, sir." His hand leaves my throat, and he steps back slightly.

"Good. My brothers should already be in the car with your stuff. We're going to get your payment from Lynal and then walk nicely out of here." I turn to the door, desperate to leave, but he moves next to my side. "But make no mistake, there is no chance of escaping. We run Seattle, and hiding bodies isn't a problem for us. So do us all a favor and behave."

I jump a little at his choice of words and have no doubt he means them. I give him a nod and pull the door open. I don't look for help. I can't have anyone hurt or dead because of me. Whatever is going to happen with the Romanos is my fate. I won't risk putting anyone else in danger to try to escape it.

I make my way to Lynal, my new captor close behind like a shadow. Lynal hands me my money hastily with fear deep in his eyes as he looks at Nico behind me. He makes no move to intervene and any final hope of a rescue dies within me.

He was the last person who might have helped me. I scan the room for Slim, thankful she isn't on the floor. She would try to help, or at least ask questions.

Making our way to the door, Nico grabs my arm, stopping us. "I can't let you walk outside like that." He shrugs off his jacket and places it over my shoulder. "Cover yourself." I instantly wrap myself in it, but I refuse to thank him for it.

He pushes the door open, and we make our way to a black SUV in the parking lot. Nico quickly helps me in the back seat where another man is sitting. He looks a lot like Nico but a little slimmer, shaggy black hair, his face showcasing a light dusting of facial hair, and he doesn't have any ear piercings. He says nothing to me, only nods at Nico and is as stiff as a damn board.

The second brother turns to look at me from the front passenger seat. He eyes me up and down, then tosses me my clothes from my cubbyhole.

"Get dressed. I don't want to drive you around looking like a whore," he commands. He's just as joyful as Nico, but I do as I am told and begin sliding on my sweatshirt over the mesh bra. No way in hell am I getting completely naked right now.

This brother has shorter hair and is clean shaven. He is just as burly as Nico, but has a snug ring in his nose. *Does he have other piercings? Shit, no Chelsey!*

They smirk as if they have just won the lottery, and I can't help but think it is hot as fuck. But I know what lies beneath those smiles. What lies below the surface in all men.

The cruel need to fuck and own anything they desire.

Chapter 2
Nico

*D*amn it, *this girl is going to be hard to live with.* I slam the door to the SUV and make my way to the driver's seat. The way she uttered 'yes sir' in there made my dick instantly hard as fucking iron.

One look at that short, curvy blond had me wanting her. That hour-glass figure with thick thighs and big tits had my cock practically begging to consume her as soon as she took the damn stage. Then her eyes locked on me and the only thing I could think about was those thick red lips around my cock with those emerald eyes staring up at me.

Then those bastards started touching her, and she rubbed her body on them and well, no one touches what's mine and she is mine whether she believes it or not.

She's lucky Marco didn't see it. The cliché middle child has the short fuse temper that goes with it. Those guys would be sporting a black eye or maybe even lost a hand if he saw them touch her.

We started looking for her simply to spite Riccardo, but Enzo and Marco saw her picture and were instantly infatuated with her. They were damn near drooling over the recon photos Enzo got and wouldn't shut up about how nice her body would feel.

Our expert hacker did all the digging on her. He's like the human version of a bloodhound, and she was his bone.

There has never been a person or information Enzo couldn't find and with the sheer lack of him looking at her right now, I know he wants to put some of the more scandalous information we found to use. Don't ask me how, but that kid even managed to find the porn videos she's watched and the vibrator order she placed last year.

But it was Marco's crazy ass idea to go pick her up.

After seeing her in person, I knew he was right. I'm being pulled to her like she has her own gravitational force. Every five seconds I'm sneaking glances at her through the rearview mirror. It's pissing me off! Women have only ever been a quick fuck, but this one is different and I already hate her for it.

Enzo is staring out the window in the backseat, too much of a gentleman to stare at her. Even though I'm sure he is daydreaming about her naked.

Chelsey, on the other hand, is fidgeting with her sweatshirt and chewing on her bottom lip, her gaze darting between us. Fuck, I can't wait to bite that lip.

Already this girl is torturing me, and she doesn't even realize it. It took every ounce of self control not to fuck her when that curvy body of hers pressed against mine. But I don't pay for pussy and I certainly don't force women to fuck me. There are plenty of men in this world who take what they please, but I have never been one of them.

Marco smirks at me with 'told you so' eyes and if he keeps it up, I'm going to knock that look off his face before the evening is out. *Asshole.*

I grip the steering wheel so tight my knuckles are white. I seriously need a shower to wash the scent of her off me before I fuckin explode. But I have a feeling this evening is far from over.

Chelsey has certainly been put through hell with a dad like David Ryan, and she has already proven she's not going to be easy and agreeable. She's been cooperative since her futile attempt to escape, but it's all a facade. I'm sure the first time one of us tries to make a move, we'll see a whole new side of fight out of her.

If Enzo's recon was right, which it always is, she has been used as a drug runner for years. Raised to hold her own, she's going to be a little hellion whenever she decides to show those claws. I am rarely wrong about these things. I have a gift of reading people and she's a damn open book.

Arriving at our building, I head to the main level garage and Chelsey's breathing quickens. She grips her sweatshirt tight like it's a lifeline that can save her. Fear radiates off her, even though she is trying like hell to hide it.

I don't blame her for hiding it. In this world fear gets you killed. You never show your weaknesses, and I'm willing to bet she knows that better than any of us.

Pulling into the spot closet to the elevator, I slam the SUV into park before climbing out. I want to watch her get out, and be there in case she tries anything stupid.

Marco climbs out next, shaking his head at me before opening the door for Chelsey, who leaves the car without any fight and follows me to the elevator, my brothers on either side of her.

I'm trying to be patient. They're simply excited to have a woman in the house again, but they need to get a grip. They are like kids at Christmas with a new damn puppy.

I place my thumbprint on the scanner above the code box, and the door opens. Chelsey enters first with trepidation, followed by Marco and Enzo on either side of her, and I enter last. The elevator seems to move at turtle speed this evening. I can hear her labored breaths, feel her shifting on her feet, but I only stare at the door.

Finally, the elevator stops, opening to the kitchen. The growing tension has me ready to burst into flames. As we shuffle out Chelsey shoves past me, whipping around to face us with her arms crossed protectively over her chest. A growl forms in my chest, but I withhold it. She's already proving to be a thorn in my side, and she already got her one free shot.

"So, it's late and I'm nasty from work. I would like a bed and a shower please," she snips at us, tossing her hair over her shoulder like she's the queen of the castle.

Apparently, the meek girl from the car has found her claws and a bit more courage to go with them.

It's going to be so fun breaking that attitude of hers. To cherry her little ass while she begs me to let her come. *Oh the plans I have for you little spitfire.* A smirk spreads across my face.

"Of course!" Enzo pipes up, shoving past me to get to her. "Come this way. I'll show you your room. I'm Enzo by the way." He gestures to her to follow him. "Your room has an attached bathroom with a soaking tub and stand-up shower. It should be stocked with everything you need." He kindly leads her down the hall, with Marco following behind her.

Rolling my eyes, I move to kitchen island that's well stocked with liquor and pour myself some of my favorite bourbon.

That boy is ever the caretaker and even though she is acting like a brat, he still is tending to her. He needs to watch himself. I have no doubt she's just biding her time with us. The only things behind her eyes are fear and anger. And I know this girl will ruin us if we let her.

Taking a large drink, I welcome the burn as it slides down my throat. I have work that needs tending to before bed and after all the shit tonight, I needed this drink.

Marco walks back into the kitchen, biting his lower lip, and rubbing his hands together.

"Dude, she's so much better looking in person!" he gawks excitedly. "Victory shots!?"

This bottle of bourbon cost me close to fifty-thousand-dollars, so he can fuck off if he thinks I'm wasting it on celebratory shots. I grab the bottle and put it away, then pin him with a cold stare.

"Oh come on man, you can't wait to have that curvy body of hers wrapped around you like a ribbon either." He makes the shape of her body with his hands and I roll my eyes.

"Marco, will you grow up please? She is nothing but a toy." I grumble before downing the rest of my bourbon. It was meant to be sipped, but I can't savor it right now. This whole situation has me tense. "Just something for us to fuck, and when we've had our fill, we send her on her way."

"Fine, you want to be an ass about this, be my guest. But just know while you're sulking, I'm going to have her screaming my name." He laughs at me, leaving me standing in the kitchen as he marches back down the hall.

Screw him. The only name I want her screaming is mine. I could have had her in that lounge room. She was completely willing to join me on that bed, but the first time I pound her into oblivion, I want her begging me for it.

I make my way through the living room and down the hall to my office, finding Enzo and Marco sitting in there waiting for me.

I drag my hand over my face and sigh. "What?" I don't know how much more shit can I take this evening before my head explodes!

Enzo stands with a stupid grin on his face. "She is set up in the guest room between your room and Marco's. She said she has everything she needs for the evening."

"Okay so is this a status update or did you two actually need something? The grown up here actually has work to do." I know they're happy she's here, but I can't keep the bite from my tone.

"Dude, knock it off!" Marco scoffs. "Can't you be a little happy she's here? I know we all get plenty of pussy from the club, but this one is ours, bro!"

I cross the room and sit down at my desk. "You two be careful with her. She's in survival mode right now. She could start acting out at any time and don't share too much about us. If this doesn't work... well I don't want to have to put her in a body bag."

"Seriously!" Enzo pipes up in outrage.

He grew up in this world, but he is only twenty-five and still has a lot to learn. If Riccardo learns we have her, there will be fall out.

And she will share whatever information she gets to save her own skin. She has no loyalty to us and will never gain any. She's a fucking hostage here.

Another sigh leaves my lips. "Why don't you two go check on our guest and make sure she isn't planning an assassination attempt on us."

"Well, there was something..." Marco grins from ear to ear.

"Seriously Marco, you're twenty-eight years old. I think you can figure out when is the appropriate time to try and fuck her is." I let my irritation fill the bite in my voice.

"No, I simply need to know if you're taking the first go?"

I roll my eyes at him. *Right.*

As the oldest and head of the Ramono Crime Family, I have the right to claim the first fuck.

"No, she's all yours boys" I wave my hand at them, dismissing them from my office. The club books are not going to do themselves and Enzo will have liquor orders to place in the next day or two.

I work well into the early morning, and there's still plenty of work that needs to get done, but I can't keep my eyes open any longer. And I can't keep that curvy blond out of my brain for more than a minute. Making sure the password lock is on, I power off the switch to my computer. I don't need our little guest helping herself to my files. She could be planning to gather information for leverage. It would be a stupid plan, but desperate people will do desperate things.

Once I get to my room, I strip down to my boxers and finally make my way to bed, her scent still in my nose.

Through the wall comes the soft whimper of tears.

Fuck me, because the only thing I want to do is go over there and wrap her in my arms. Tell her she is safe here with us. That I will destroy anyone who tries to hurt a single hair on her head while she is mine, and she is mine until I decide otherwise.

Chapter 3
Chelsey

The night stretched on and I was left completely alone. I thought once they brought me here, I would be expected to fuck them to their heart's desires. But no one came. I sigh, thankful for the small bit of peace before the storm that is sure to come.

I don't want to leave the sanctuary that is my room this morning. I'm not sure what to expect from my new captors, so avoiding them is the best I can come up with at the moment.

The large room has a king bed with a beautiful fully stocked vanity in the corner next to the door for the walk-in closet. Across from the bed sits a large, long dresser filled with clothes and lingerie, all in my size. I guess Nico wasn't kidding when he said they did recon on me. But really it feels more like a lion stalking their prey, and I'm just a helpless gazelle.

How the hell am I going to get out of here? I didn't risk my life to rid myself of one devil just to be owned by another. And I'm not going to be a guest with no expectations forever.

I have no interest belonging to anyone. I want my freedom.

I've been barely surviving at the club and I refuse to let all that struggle be for nothing.

I need a plan. Before coming to Seattle, I spent a little time in Arizona. I bet I could find work pretty easy in Phoenix-

A knock on the door has me rushing to sit on the bed. It's a little strange, but I feel safer sitting on the bed rather than standing face to face with whoever is knocking.

It's rare I ever get the curtsey of a knock and I didn't expect my captors to be the ones to give it to me.

"Come in," my voice is filled with fake confidence as anxiety swirls in my gut and my palms begin to sweat, but I hold my head high.

The brother from the front seat walks in with a tray holding coffee and a plate of pancakes and sausage. He looks different in the late-morning light. Easily six-foot-two, tattoos cover his sculpted, muscular arms. He is like a sexy, threatening playboy that knows he could make any woman swoon for him.

The playboy approaches me with a mischievous glint in his eyes and holy shit, the food smells incredible. I haven't eaten anything since the small salad lunch yesterday. I didn't want to be bloated for work. Not that I had much else for food in the house anyway. Only living on the cash from the club made things difficult.

He sets the tray on the bed next to me, then sits on the corner away from me. Like he's trying to give me space, and make me comfortable. Almost like I'm a stray dog and he needs to gain my trust.

Jokes on him, I don't trust anyone. Slim was the only person I ever let close, and she didn't even know my real name or anything about my past. *Shit. I hope she's okay.*

Hopefully she's not freaking out about me leaving without saying goodbye. Maybe I can convince her to come to Phoenix with me once I get out of here. We can start over together. Hell, maybe someday I'll actually find a man worthy of a romance novel. If they actually exist.

My stomach rumbles at the smell of the food, but the small voice in my head can't help but be on edge. *This is too kind for ownership. What if it's drugged? What's the motive here? Feed me and then fuck me? Torture me for information I don't have?*

"You're hungry. I heard your stomach from here." I gaze up at him, making no move to take the food. "I promise it doesn't come with any expectations, and it's not drugged."

His warm smile begs me to believe him. *So, I'm no longer the whore from last night huh?* I raise my eyebrows at him.

Rolling his eyes, he leans over and takes a sip of coffee. Then tears off a piece of the pancake and eats it.

"There satisfied?" He moves back to the corner and gestures towards the tray. "Now eat Little Bird, you're hungry and we both know it."

I guess it can't be drugged if he ate it. And his promise of no expectations means I can fight like hell if he tries to break that without consequences from Nico.

The first bite of food tastes like heaven. Pancakes were never in my diet because of the carbs. But when I was little, before my body was used for the pleasure of others, my mother used to make them all the time for me. My heart aches a little at the memory, but I shove it down.

A small moan escapes me on my next bite and I blush. The playboy chuckles and smiles to himself, staring at his feet.

"Thank you for the food. I was pretty hungry, and these pancakes are good," I mumble, chewing on my breakfast.

"Of course, we have no intention of starving you." He looks up, smiling at me once again. *Fuck, that smile is sexy.* "My name is Marco, and I'm glad you like the pancakes. It was my morning to cook breakfast." He shifts a little closer and heat pools between my thighs.

33

What is wrong with me? He might be hot as hell, but he kidnapped you and is currently holding you prisoner. He's no better than my father's men.

"Well, thank you. Pancakes are one of my favorites and it's been a long time since I have had some," I say before taking another bite.

"Favorite huh? Am I going to be the favorite one off of principle then?" He smirks.

"Maybe," I coo. "Are you going to bring me expectation free pancakes every morning?"

His grin spreads and I yearn to kiss those soft lips of his.

"If I get to be the favorite, then I'll do more than just bring you pancakes for breakfast, Little Bird." His eyes darken and my thighs clench together.

I want to shoot back a snarky comeback, but my brain freezes. *You can't flirt with him, or be rude.* It's a sure way to get myself into more trouble than I can handle.

I stuff more pancake in my mouth, avoiding a response, but my cheeks heat slightly. Marco chuckles, returning his gaze back to the floor.

"Thank you for the food." I say kindly once I'm done.

"You're welcome." Marco stands, then grabs the tray. I watch as he sets it on the dresser, then comes to sit next to me. My pulse skyrockets and I force my breathing to stay steady.

"You said you had no expectations." I snap, pinning him with my eyes. I should have known better than to trust a man at his word. It doesn't matter how tempting and attractive he is, no man has the right to touch me anymore...

"Relax, I'm not here to fuck you. I just want to get to know you." There's a defensive edge to his tone.

My eyes widen and it takes all my effort not to allow my jaw to fall open. "No one has ever just wanted to get to know me. Usually they fuck me, then say they'll be back for another round in a bit."

Marco cocks his head slightly and sits up straighter, like I've said something odd as my words hang for a moment. Eventually I relax just a little, realizing he means what he said.

"Why do you want to know me?" I ask, eyebrows furrowing together and shaking my head at him.

He shrugs and lets out a breath. "You're worth more than just being something to stick my cock in. If I wanted that, there are plenty of whores at the club we own."

I don't understand what his angle is, he has to have other motives.

"If you have no desire to have me in bed, then why am I here?"

I can't meet his gaze as I ask the question. I don't want to push him, and this feels like playing with fire, but I nothing has made sense since I got out of that car.

"Look at me." His commanding bark has more heat flooding between my thighs, and I follow his command. "I never said I didn't want you in bed. All I said was, I want to know you and that you're worth more than your pussy." He rake's a hand through his hair and shoves me back on to the bed.

He quickly towers over me and my heart feels like it's about to beat right out of my chest. "If you would like me to show you how much I desire you, I can fuck you until you're a trembling mess, right here right now." My breathing shakes, adrenaline pulsing in my veins as my pussy throbs with need. "But if you don't want that, I would love to learn more about you." A wicked smirk covers his face as he hovers over me.

His crass words have me flushed with need and I press my thighs closer together attempting to soothe my needy sex. I should hate him but yet, my body is screaming to feel all of him.

I haven't been with anyone since leaving my dad's gang. Never had the desire to, but holy shit do I want this man.

Marco stares at me intently, never making a move one way or another. The sexual tension building between us getting stronger by the second.

I could fuck him because I want to right? He's giving me a choice here.

It's wrong that I find myself wanting him, but a strong, powerful, sexy man has me pinned to the bed and is actually giving me a choice. I could tell him no and he would get off me without complaint — hello romance novel! But I don't know if I want him to.

"So, Little Bird..." He gives me a tempting smile. "Am I getting to know you or am I getting you naked?"

"If I get naked with you..." the words come out completely breathless. "Will I be expected to do it again, or with the other men in this house?"

"No, you may be our little hostage but we don't force women into our beds. Our momma raised us right."

"No, you just kidnap them instead. Coerce them into being your fuck toys with those pretty eyes and rippling muscles," I bite at him. I need the anger and frustration to override the desperate need to be naked with him right now.

"You're only a fuck toy if you allow us to fuck you, and if we didn't take you, Riccardo would have been along soon enough." He levels me with his gaze. "So yes, we were raised right."

As soon as the words leave his mouth, I give up on fighting my desire and kiss him, hard.

What the hell, I've fucked plenty of men out of obligation. For once I have an opportunity to do it because I want to. If I'm their new toy, I may as well get my pleasure and enjoy them as my toys too.

Marco springs into action, immediately taking off my shirt, quickly followed by his. There is nothing gentle about the way we kiss each other, only lust and need.

His tongue invades my mouth, claiming every inch of it. He tastes like a smooth bourbon, and I wonder if he took a shot before coming in here. Leaving my mouth, he kisses down my neck to my breasts. Sucking and biting every inch of the way.

I'm ready to explode as he sucks one of my hard peaks into his mouth. Moaning, I arch into him as he grinds his hard cock into my sex.

"Holy fuck ..." I whimper.

"Oh there's nothing holy about what I'm going to do to you, Little Bird."

My sex throbs at his words and I'm sure my panties are soaked. I want more, no I need more.

I move my hands over his firm, built arms, down his chiseled chest, and over his defined abs, before I grab the top of his pants.

He takes hold of me, stopping me from removing his pants. "Eager, are we?" His husky voice has me ready to beg for him. "I'm not done playing with you yet." He groans as he covers my lips again. God, this man claims my mouth like he was starved for me.

He sits up in a jerk and removes my pants, leaving completely bare before him. He stares at my body. His eyes trailing over my breasts, across my abdomen, to the apex of my thighs.

"Get the hell out of here you fat fuck! Go get me someone suitable!" The memory of one of my dads men flashes through my brain.

Anxiety swirls in my gut as his eyes drink me in and slowly, I begin to cover myself.

I have so much on my love handles, definitely missing a thigh gap, and my stomach is far from perfect. I don't like living in the past, but the idea of him rejecting me because of my body has me anxious and unsure.

"Stop," he orders. "You are exquisite, and you will not hide yourself from me. Your body is flawless, and it is mine. Do you understand?" His words make the voices of the past vanish. They make my body sing.

"Yes..."

"Good girl." His gaze never leaves my body as he pulls down his pants, allowing his cock to spring free.

My mouth instantly dries. His cock his fucking huge! It stands thick and long, with a wicked dydoe piercing and a bead of pre-cum.

I have never been with a pierced guy before... I bet it will feel like heaven.

Dragging my eyes from his glorious cock, I take in the full sleeve tattoo running the length of his left arm and up over his shoulder, my eyes landing back on his dangerous appendage.

"Why don't you come lick it like you're dying to, Little Bird?" he growls.

I don't hesitate. I get on my knees and run my tongue over the tip of him, then down his length.

He hisses as I take him in my mouth, moving up and down, every pump hitting the back of my throat. I'm unable to take all of him, so I wrap my hand around his hilt.

"Fuck, you suck my cock so good," his husky voice praises as his fingers lace through my hair.

It fuels me to keep going, to take him deeper down my throat. Tears spring to my eyes as he chokes me, and determination settles in. I will be the best he has ever had. I pump and pump eager to taste him as he spills down my throat.

"My turn." He pulls me back, shoving me from his cock before I get the chance. "I'm ready to see if that pussy of yours tastes as good as it smells." He groans pulling me under him. Fuck, this is wild and chaotic, but boy am I here for it!

Lifting my legs over his shoulders, he runs his tongue through my slick folds.

"Fuck, Marco!" My head lulls to the side as pleasure consumes me.

Eventually I open my eyes, making eye contact with Nico leaning against the wall, a straining bulge in his pants. *What the fuck!* When the hell did he walk in here?

I squirm and tense, but Marco places his hand on my abdomen holding me still. I feel dirty under Nico's stare, as his brother thoroughly enjoys my pussy.

"Eyes on me Little Bird." Marco's growl vibrates against my pussy. "He's just jealous that I am between your thighs, and he isn't. He won't touch you, but let's let him enjoy the show."

I move my gaze back to Marco and his tongue is intoxicating. He circles my clit then slides his fingers into my entrance. I build and build, as he works me expertly.

"That's it come for me," Marco praises. "And eyes on me when you do."

I do as he says and with two more strokes I tip over the edge.

"Oh Shit..." I yell as he works me through my climax. My eyes roll to the back of my head at the sheer intensity of it.

"How does she taste?" Nico's husky voice groans.

"So damn sweet, like a summer peach."

Nico's groan is joined by another.

My eyes shoot back to the wall, where Enzo leans next to Nico. My eyes lock on him and he smirks.

"You come so beautifully on my brother's face, Sweet Peach." Enzo makes heat flood me.

"She likes your praise bro. She just got even more soaked." Marco groans.

Why is this so damn hot?

The rational part of my brain is begging me to find this horrifying, but I'm only that much more turned on. I'm a god damn queen right now.

"Now eyes back to me." I follow the command. "This time when I make you come. I want to hear my name on your lips."

Marco climbs over me, and my breathing hitches as I feel him nudging my entrance.

"You ready for me, Little Bird?"

"Yes... I haven't been with anyone in a while... go easy on me."

Marco fills me slowly, one inch at a time as my pussy stretches to take him. I've been with a good amount of guys, but none have been as big as Marco.

He stills for a moment, allowing me to adjust to his presence.

"Fuuuck, your pussy is so damn tight." He growls in my ear. "That was the only gentle you're going to get from me. Tell me when you're ready."

Now! I start to wiggle under him and without warning he pounds into me HARD.

Oh God. I crave every powerful thrust and rock against him as he quickens his pace. He is just as lost in this as I am. I thought I wanted gentle, but he is working me expertly, like he knows that's not what I needed.

My walls start to quake as I claw at his back.

"That's it come around my cock like a good girl."

His words are my undoing and I shatter under him, coming harder than the last one. "AH Marco!"

"Fuck!" he bellows spilling into me with his own release. My pussy is still pulsing around his cock, when he invades my mouth with his tongue again.

"You're so greedy. Your pussy milked my cock till there wasn't a drop left."

I moan at his words.

I'm nothing but a limp shell and he rolls to the side of me tucking me into his chest. I've NEVER had sex like that before. The pleasure, the intensity, the desire, it was all out of this damn world!

Marco makes no move to leave, he is snuggling me. Tears start to well in me, no one has ever snuggled me. Men usually take their release and leave. *You will not cry in front of them. You will not show weakness.*

The bed shifts as Nico and Enzo sit at the edge. But I'm so boneless that I don't care that they are here.

"I have a warm cloth for you. May I?" Enzo's voice is soothing.

He just asked me permission. I don't think I have ever felt like it was my permission to give before today. He doesn't move, just waits for me to respond. I can't talk or I may actually start to cry. So, I give him the only thing I have, a simple nod.

He takes my permission and cleans me up, but never touches me outside of the warm cloth. Once he's done, Enzo and Nico move off the bed and leave the room. Marco begins to move and release me as well, but I cling to him.

Snuggling me back to him, he covers us with a blanket. This is new and overwhelming, but as sleep threatens to take me, I feel so cherished by all of them.

Chapter 4
Marco

Holy fucking shit, Chesley is better than anything I could have dreamt for. She took everything I gave her without missing a beat and when she saw my brothers watching, she was still all in with me. She enjoyed that as much as I did, and I think it scared her a little.

We've only shared a woman twice, and neither lasted long. We were too much to handle, but with how Chelsey handled my brothers watching I can already tell this is going to be different. Neither of the others would allow us to all participate together. Nic was resistant to the idea of bring in Chelsey at first, but I know he is warming to her already. He wouldn't have been in there if he wasn't.

Them watching as I fucked our girl, was so damn invigorating. They wanted her so bad, but I was the one that got her. Pride fills my chest knowing she gave herself to me. *I. Got. Her.*

The high noon light shines through the windows, but Chelsey is sound asleep in my arms. She's just as beautiful when she sleeps and looks genuinely peaceful. I don't think she realizes how beautiful she actually is. Every inch of her is perfect. Her smooth skin, juicy ass, long silky hair, is a walking wet dream. Though I will definitely be asking Enzo about the large scar across her back. And why he never said anything about it when we reviewed her medical records.

Slowly, I move off the bed and retrieve my clothes. It would be nice to watch her sleep the day away, but I'm sure

Nic is brooding and that I have yet to get any work done for the day.

Once I'm dressed, I steal a final glance at my Little Bird in the bed, grab the tray, and close the door softly behind me. I don't really give a shit if Nic is mad about me fucking Chelsey, but I still like to know where I stand.

Making my way through the house, I drop the dishes in the sink, and head to Nic's office. If I'm the target of his wrath it's important I'm mentally prepared for all the extra work he is going to dole out to me. He likes to work us to the bone when we fuck up.

As I walk in to his large office, Enzo is on the couch in the corner playing on his phone while Nic is sitting behind his large desk staring at his computer screen with a scowl.

"Good, you finally left her." Nic looks up at me. "We need to discuss something." His voice is firm and commanding like always.

"What's up?" I ask, leaning on the wall with my arms crossed over my chest. Readying myself for a lecture about how she has been here less than twenty-four-hours and I've already bedded her.

"I don't think Chelsey has ever been asked permission before when it comes to her body," Enzo starts.

What the hell? It would be more obvious wouldn't it? Like her being fucking terrified of sex. No way she would have allowed me to fuck her back there.

Is that what that scar is from, did someone give it to her?

"And what gave you that idea?" My eyes are daggers at my brother.

"We knew her dad had her working for him for years and that he had every intention to sell her to Riccardo as a concubine." He pauses, looking almost sad. "But the fear her eyes held when she saw us watching, and the way her whole body tensed when I asked to touch her." Shifting forward in his seat, he purses his lips like he is mulling over his own words. "It took a long time for her to respond, man. Almost like she didn't know how to."

My blood begins to boil at the idea that the girl in the other room, *my* girl, has been raped repeatedly for years. Is that how she lost her virginity? Was it stolen from her? Fuck I hate that he's right. The way she reacted to me wanting to know her. The questions she asked me. The way she held in her tears when I snuggled her after.

"Her dad isn't mafia, only a head of a gang," I sneer. "Let's go take that piece of shit out! He doesn't deserve to be breathing if he did what you're suggesting!" I push off the wall with my fist clenched at my side.

I'm one of the heads of the Romano Crime Family, and if I want someone dead, they die.

"Marco, that's enough!" Nic's voice booms as he stands from his seat, planting both hands on his desk. "David is under Riccardo's protection, and we don't even know for sure if that is the truth. We need Chelsey to confirm it as fact, plus I'm not prepared for an all out war with Riccardo over her."

"Nico, she is ours and she has a large scar across her back that is probably from him," I growl.

She's supposed to be a toy, a means to an end, but I already find myself not wanting to let her go. She is mine, and I'll protect her as such.

"We cannot help what happened to her before she was with us, we can only take care of her now." Enzo rests a hand on my shoulder, his voice is calm like a smooth melody. "But what scar are you talking about? None of her medical records said anything about a major scar?" He looks at me genuinely confused.

Why does he always feel the need to be the peacekeeper between my brother and I? It's annoying.

"There is a massive fucking scar on her back, Enzo!" I yell, punching the door to relieve some of these feelings, but not hard enough to bust it. "And if it's not on any medical reports, David fucking Ryan probably did it himself! I'm going to kill the bastard!"

"MARCO! Get a grip! You fucked her once and your acting like she is your whole damn world! Get your shit together!" Nic's commanding boss voice comes out. "If you can't handle her being here, I'll have her out of here by the end of the night."

His threat lands its mark.

"Whatever, I need some air." Shoving Enzo's hand off me and moving past him, I leave the office and head to shower. I need to think, I need to get the image of my girl being raped out of my head, of her screaming and begging for them to stop. Of her laying on a floor feeling lifeless.

The hot water beats my muscles and usually melts stress away, but the thought of Chelsey being treated that way has me ready to kill anyone who has ever touched her. But Nic's right, we can't start a war on a suspicion. Even though, if given the chance, that is exactly what I would do. Riccardo is a prick who has been a menace since his reign over the Italian Mafia began, and David is a low level monster.

Riccardo would have to be a clean kill—fast so no rescue could be made, but David...

I could string him up in the basement by his wrists, just high enough so his toes barely touch the ground. I could remove each of his fingers, cauterizing the wound in between so he couldn't bleed out, and when I got tired of his screams, I could remove his tongue. Continuing my slow torture until I was satisfied. Only then would I give him the sweet release of death.

Shutting off the shower, I realize my imagination is doing nothing to help wash away the anger and tension rolling through me. So I force my brain to focus on work instead. Our order should have been delivered by now, so I can go help stock. Then Nic can meet me at the club and help run security this evening. Moving to my closet, I get dressed in one of my suits and prepare to go to the club for the evening.

Work will be simple tonight unless Mark has a drug dealer that has been causing trouble for me to deal with.

We don't move drugs, our hands are clean. But we do oversee this city and when the pimps or drug dealers step over the line, it's my job to deal with them.

Nic is the head, and manages our club and business affairs. Enzo deals with the daily workings of the club and hacks and tracks. I'm the muscle and second in command. I'd be lying if I said I didn't like getting my hands dirty. Breaking bones, forcing information out of people, watching them bleed, it gives me a level of satisfaction that nothing else ever has. Part of me hopes someone needs a beating tonight, simply so I can work out this anger I feel.

Once I'm ready for the evening, I leave my room and head to Chelsey. But the guest room's door is still shut. I want to check on her, but space is probably best. This is still new for all of us.

No one wanted to leave her alone in the apartment tonight either. So we agreed Enzo would be the first to stay back with her. I wanted to protest, I wanted it to be me. But I conceded because he is the more empathetic one and women can be sensitive. He can help with her emotional needs better than I would be able to. Certainly better than Nic would be able to.

"I'm going down to the club. Enjoy the evening off with Chelsey." I wink at my little brother as I enter the kitchen.

"Oh I plan to. I picked out a great movie, and I got all the snacks." His cocky excitement has me a little jealous.

I walk over to him and slug him in the shoulder. "Don't touch my Oreos."

"If the lady wants them, who am I to deny her?" He shrugs, and a grin spreads across his face. That was a no room for argument answer and he knows it. The shit head may even offer them to her just so he can eat them.

"AHHHH NO STOP!" Chelsey's blood-curdling scream fills the apartment.

SHIT! Enzo and I don't miss a beat, running to her room. The screams don't stop and it's like we are moving in slow motion.

Our apartment has top-notch security and it should be absolutely impossible for someone to get in here without us knowing. But her screams make me second guess everything.

Nic beats us to her door and goes barging in, Enzo and I close behind.

Chelsey's screams don't stop, but when we enter the room, she is alone. Still in bed sleeping, but thrashing about and covered in sweat.

We all stare at her; no one making a move. You're not supposed to wake someone having a night terror episode, but fuck this is hard to watch. My chest aches at the sight and I cross my arms over myself.

Enzo is the first to move towards the bed. Nic and I closely follow as we all take a seat on her bed. She screams a few more times. I want to look at the floor, to rid myself of witnessing her torment, but how can I? This is the only thing I can do, just watch and wait. Releasing another scream, she jolts awake.

The pure terror in her eyes makes my heart ache. She scrambles on the bed, clutching the blanket like a lifeline, her eyes darting around the room.

"Shhh, Sweet Peach. You're safe," Enzo soothes, leaning slightly towards her.

Her gaze locks with his and I watch as the fear changes into something else and she begins to sob uncontrollably.

Chapter 5

Enzo

Chelsey's tears are like a knife to my chest. She has been so strong and refused to show her fear and weaknesses since getting here, but whatever her dream was, it broke her.

I don't care if it's what I should do or not, but I refuse to watch her face this alone. Climbing closer to her on the bed, I wrap my arms around her and pull her to my chest. She stiffens, but I pretend not to notice and start rubbing soothing circles on her back.

For a moment, I question if this was a mistake, but it only takes a few seconds for her to turn into my chest and sob into my shirt.

Her body relaxes a bit in my arms and I'm thankful for it. The last thing I want is to make this worse for her.

Marco is staring at me with gratitude and longing filling his eyes, but Nic looks bewildered. He's never been much of a comforter, but right now he looks like an alien just landed in front of him. We all sit in silence, listening to the broken sobs coming from this small creature.

Chelsey begins to calm, and after a moment she pulls away. I miss her warmth instantly, but force myself to refrain from pulling her back to me.

"I'm so sorry. I completely ruined your shirt." She covers her face with her hands.

"It's okay, I don't mind." I smile and catch her eyes. "Are you okay?"

She doesn't answer for a long moment, and I watch as she tries to piece herself together.

"Yeah, I'm good. My emotions just got the best of me." Her voice is filled with fake enthusiasm. If that is all she's willing to give me right now, I'll take it until she's ready to share.

"Cut the crap." Nic's commanding voice booms, pulling us from our bubble. "Chelsey you were screaming at the top of your lungs in your sleep. Don't lie to us and say you're good."

Marco and I look at him with complete *"what the fuck"* expressions. Now is not the time for his harsh and gruff demeanor.

"I was talking to Enzo." Chelsey snaps at him. Her eyes are daggers. "Not you." Shit, this girl may have balls bigger than any of the guys we have working for us.

Nic could have steam shooting out of his ears with the rage covering him at her blatant dismissal of him.

Shooting forward, he pinches her cheeks in his hand. "You will not dismiss me like that. You will not forget that You. Are. Mine." His words are a growl and I expect Chelsey to shrink away, but she doesn't. Instead she presses into him and not a single ounce of her deadly stare softens. "Tell me what caused you to have a night terror right now."

She is firm and unwavering and growls back at him. "Fuck off, jack-ass." Then rips out of his grasp and smacks him hard across the face with a loud clap.

Oh fuck...

I'm not sure if I'm terrified for her life or proud of her for standing up to him. This is like sliding on ice while driving. You see the light turn red and the car coming into the intersection, but no matter how much you try you can't stop the collision. I knew Chelsey had a fiery side but holy hell.

Nico turns beat red and his fist clenched at his side. I've seen him kill people for less.

"Okay. Okay. Nic we have a shift at the club." Marco grabs him and starts dragging him to the door, but his eyes never leave hers. "Enzo, make sure she's good. I'll see you later," Marco shouts from the doorway as it clicks shut.

Only then do I release the breath I was holding. I trust that my brother can calm him down.

No one, and I mean no one, has ever hit Nic and lived to tell about it. But the balls this woman has to actually slap him... I'm impressed to say the least.

With Nic gone, I really do need to make sure she's okay.

"I'm sorry Nic was so rude to you. He was just worried about you. Just like Marco and I." I brush her hair from her face, the fire still burning deep in her eyes. "We had to sit here and wait for you to wake up, while you screamed like you were being murdered... It was hard to stomach."

"He didn't have to be so demanding!" she yells, tension radiating off her in thick waves. "I may be a prisoner, but that doesn't give him the right to know everything I've been through! He doesn't fucking own me!"

I let her words sit for a minute, watching as the anger crumbles away back to the hurt she was facing before Nic got involved.

"So do you want to tell me what you dreamt about?" I ask, raising an eyebrow at her.

A half smile brushes her face and she fiddles with her fingers. The silence kills me as she ponders her response.

I want to know what tortured her, want her to feel safe and share it with me. I want her to know that I'll take care of her. But if she isn't ready for that, I won't force her.

"Can we- I'm sorry. I don't want to make you mad." Her voice is unsure.

This is the same woman mere minutes ago slapped the true head of our crime family, yet she's worried about making a choice for herself. She is a puzzle I can't figure out.

"We can do what you want," I reassure her, running a thumb over her cheek gently.

"Well, can we just go watch a movie and pretend none of this happened?" She looks up at me with weary eyes, gauging my reaction to her avoiding my question.

"I can't guarantee that the others will let this go, but for tonight, we sure can, Sweet Peach."

"Thank you" She smiles and I squeeze her hand reassuringly. She's not okay, but at least we are taking steps in the right direction.

"I'll go get things set up." I pat her leg as I stand and head out the door. Allowing her space to stitch together her internal wounds that were just all too exposed.

Making my way to the kitchen, I can't help the bounce in my step. I'm excited to spend some time with Chelsey. My recon showed me a bunch of things, but there are things even the best tech person can't find and those are the things I want to know.

I set out popcorn, Marco's Oreos, a bag of potato chips, and a Black Cherry Mikes Hard Lemonade on the coffee table in the living room. Aquaman is set up and waiting to be played, and I'm chilling here in a t-shirt with my gray sweatpants when Chelsey walks in.

Her blonde hair is down and beautifully wavy when it's wet, and she is wearing a thin strapped tank top and cotton shorts that barely cover her backside.

As soon as I lay eyes on her, I have to shift to hide my growing erection, because I've never seen a sexier woman.

"Come sit. I got snacks and have the movie set and ready." I offer her a friendly smile. She stands just outside the living room, fiddling with the edge of her shit. She looks like she is still uncomfortable, like she is waiting for the shoe to drop, but there is no shoe. At least not with me or Marco.

Eventually she saunters over to the couch and takes a seat at the opposite end, looking over the coffee table filled with stuff. I couldn't find any details on snack preferences when I did my recon, so I did the best I could.

"How did you know Mike's Black Cherry was my drink of choice?" she asks hesitantly reaching to grab the bottle.

"Expert recon guy, remember?" I tilt my head. "There were a few pictures of you at clubs and every time you had a Mike's Black Cherry in your hand." She shrinks away a little at the reminder that I half stalked her. "But I couldn't find anything on snack choices. So, I got a little of everything. What do you think of the snacks?"

A small smile spreads across her face and a blossom of hope warms my chest that this evening might actually go well.

"All the snacks look great, but do you have any peanut butter to go with the Oreos?"

"Peanut butter, huh? Yeah I'll be right back." Her small smile gets bigger and I jump off the couch. That smile of hers is awe-inspiring, and it could bring me to my knees.

Marco is going to be so annoyed about the Oreos, but I don't really care. If the thought of them with peanut butter brings that huge glowing smile to her face, I'll steal his cookies every damn day until he kills me and puts me in an early grave.

When I return to the couch, she shoots forward snatching the package of cookies then lathers a thick layer of peanut butter over the top of one.

"Oh my god," she groans around the cookie in her mouth.

A chuckle escapes me, and her cheeks turn the prettiest hue of pink. "That good, huh?" I question with a smirk.

"Have you never had an Oreo with peanut butter before?" she asks like it's an outrageous thing. A true crime to humanity.

I shake my head and it takes her a whole five seconds to shove a cookie with peanut butter at me, grinning bigger than a man who won the lottery.

How could I deny her with a smile like that?

I eat the cookie and she waits for my response with bouncing enthusiasm.

"It's really good. This might become my new favorite way to eat these cookies."

"Umm try the only way to eat these cookies."

We laugh in unison as she slides closer to me.

"So are you ready to watch the best superhero movie ever?" I gesture to the screen and her eyebrows pinch together.

"I've never actually seen a superhero movie. Dad never allowed me to watch much TV." It's a small bit, but it's something about her life she was willing to share with me and I feel honored that she did.

"Well prepare to be amazed, because Aquaman is the best!"

She chuckles then snuggles into my side as I hit play on the movie.

Chelsey is captivated by the movie. The same movie I'm not paying any attention to.

No, my focus is on the beautiful, sexy woman leaning into my side. My dick has been painfully hard since she moved in close, but the last thing I want is to ruin the good thing we're forming by trying to get her naked.

We finish the movie snuggled close, and I don't think there is a happier man on planet Earth than I am at this moment.

Chapter 6
Chelsey

The movie night with Enzo is a perfect evening and I rarely get those. With him I feel peaceful, like I could share pieces of me without getting burned. He seems more of a friend rather than a captor. I know he's here to keep me from running away, but in a way, it feels like he is also here because he wants to be.

The warmth of his arms has been a peaceful place for me to melt into during the movie and now that it's over, I don't want to leave them. A yawn escapes me as I snuggle into his chest further, savoring the feel of him and the little piece of bliss we're in.

I feel like all I've done since getting here is sleep, but I haven't slept without the fear of being found in months. The stress and anxiety, plus always having to be looking over my shoulder was exhausting. And in a weird way, being kidnapped means I don't have to do that now, or at least didn't until I slapped Nico, but that asshole had it coming.

"So now that the movie is done, should I turn on something else, or are you ready for bed?" Enzo's silky voice asks, as he tucks a stand of hair behind my ear not resting on his chest.

"I don't want to leave the couch with you, but I'm exhausted. I don't think I could stay awake another ten-minutes into a show." Another yawn escapes me as I finish the sentence and Enzo's chest vibrates with a silent chuckle.

"Let's get you to bed then." He begins to shift me off him and the reality of his words hits me like a brick.

He's not sending me to bed and staying here, but taking me to bed. Anxiety swirls in my belly and my heart rate quickens. I thought tonight was just us hanging out, but deep down I know that's not how this world works. Now that he has taken care of me, I'm expected to take care of him.

Nothing is ever free. I was fooling myself thinking this nice evening would be.

Enzo walks with me into my room and takes a seat on the bed as I walk to the vanity. I can feel his stare, but I need a minute. Staring at my reflection, I try to prepare myself for what comes next.

A woman is only as good as her pussy... You have taken care of plenty of men. He is just one more. Get it over with and you can go to sleep.

With that last thought, I push away from the vanity and turn to face Enzo. He is staring at me, his eyebrows pinched together, mouth flat, examining my face.

Don't worry, I know my role here. I won't make you force me. It's all the words I want to say but don't.

I meet his gaze and peel off my shirt, allowing my large boobs to bounce free.

71

Enzo immediately jumps off the bed and crosses the room, stopping in front of me. "What are you doing?" His voice is deep and firm.

Warning bells ring in my head that I've done something wrong, but I have no clue what.

"You gave me a great evening and then brought me to bed. I assumed you had normal male expectations." I press my body into his, but he jumps back and holds up his hands.

"Damn it Chelsey! No!" I flinch at his sudden angry tone, his voice booming. "I have done everything this evening to be nice, to get to know you, to spend time with you. To TAKE CARE OF YOU!" He rakes a hand through his hair and his other lands on his hip. "Chelsey, I don't want your obligation fuck. You're worth so much more than that. The only time I want to fuck you is when you want me to!"

My eyes widened in shock as the reality of his words hit me. He's really upset that I thought he expected this.

"Just go to bed Chelsey. Good night." He turns on his heels and leaves, slamming the door behind him.

I jump at the bang of the door and tears well in my eyes. The reality of how badly I upset him is shocking. I was wrong.

These men don't want me to do anything out of force or obligation. The total opposite of every other man I've known.

Guilt pangs in my chest. *I ruined a great evening.*

Marco gave me a choice, Enzo took care of me, and even though he is being the biggest dick, Nico had concern all over him when he yelled at me. These men care about me... not my body, not how I can care for their sexual needs. For once, just me being me is enough.

Silent tears stream down my face as Enzo walks back in. He snatches a blanket off the bed and gently wraps it around me.

"I'm sorry for yelling, my Sweet Peach." He pulls me into a hug and holds me against his chest. "As long as you're here, you'll never be forced or expected to do anything with your body you don't want to." His voice is soothing and reassuring, and instinctively I melt into his strong arms once more.

"I'm learning that..." I sniffle and bat a stray tear away. "Thank you for this evening."

"Of course, now let's get you to bed." He releases me from his hug and walks me to the bed.

"Zo, will you stay with me and just hold me like you did on the couch?"

A small smile dusts his face, and it warms my insides. *Maybe I didn't ruin our evening.*

"Sure."

Climbing into the bed next to me, he wraps his arms around me and the soothing thump of his heart makes all my feelings feel not so big. "Zo huh? I like it..." His voice is back to the smooth melody from earlier.

Nestling my face into his chest is the only response I have. I'm thankful he's here with me right now, and a small spark of joy blooms inside. I feel at peace once again in his arms and a soft smile forms on my face. Right now there is nowhere else I would rather be.

• • • ● ● • ● ● • • •

"You stupid bitch! You didn't give me a son, so you will not block me from my daughter!" My dad's voice booms with anger followed by the sound of glass shattering. I need to run. *I have to run or he will catch me.*

Mommy told me he was a bad man now, and that's why we had to leave. She said I wasn't safe.

"No, David! You can't have her. I will die before I let you take her!" Mom's voice shrieks.

"Have it your way, bitch!" He growls ignoring her sobs as the shot fills the air.

"Mommy no!" I burst from the closet. She told me to stay put, but Daddy can't kill Mommy. I have to stop him.

"Chelsey wake up! You're having a bad dream!" Zo's voice jolts me awake.

My breathing is heavy as I take in my surroundings. I'm in the guest room, I'm in the bed, with Zo. I'm okay. I'm safe.

"It was just a dream. You're okay." His voice soothes me, but it wasn't just a dream. The memory from when I was six lingers. *When my life changed forever.* Hollowness fills me.

"Zo, can you help me with something?"

"Anything, what do you need?" He sits up to meet my gaze.

"I need to forget..." *I need to feel you.* Need to escape the memories. Need to erase my mother's sobs from my mind.

Zo will treat me with care and make me feel good. And I need him to fuck me until all of the horrible, empty feelings are gone. Until I can escape into pleasure and pretend it was nothing more than a nightmare.

"Okay?" He looks down at me with confusion and concern.

But instead of using words, I reach up and kiss him. Slowly, softly, hopeful he understands what I'm asking for.

He doesn't deepen the kiss or move to touch me, but he doesn't break it either. I'm driving this right now and I don't want that.

Pulling back I look him in the eye. "Zo, I need you to take care of me, please. Make me feel something more than a hollow pit." A war etches his face as he decides what to do. "Please, after that dream. I need to feel alive." I see the moment he decides and a sense of relief floods me.

"I'll take care of you, Sweet Peach," he coos, cupping my cheek softly.

He leans down and kisses me, taking it deeper than before. He moves with such grace, as he shifts to hover over me and I run my fingers through his thick black hair. It's as smooth as the finest silk.

His hands slide down the length of my body then come back up to my breast.

Fireworks explode across my skin and I arch into him, seeking more.

He caresses me, then moves to my other breast, treating them with such gentle care.

Slowly, savoring the feel of him, I remove his shirt. Then rub my hands down his sculpted back. He groans then pulls back from me.

"Are you sure about this?" Concern still on his face as his eyes search mine.

"Yes, please don't stop," I whimper, leaning back up to meet his lips once more.

After a moment, he moves back, sitting back on his heels. He slowly removes my shorts and panties and immediately runs two fingers through my slick fold. Staring at my center, he slides two fingers into my entrance.

Moaning at his delicious intrusion, I'm ready to burst into flames, but he quickly removes them. My gaze meets his lust filled eyes, as he slides his fingers into his mouth. *Shit, that was so sexy.*

"Hmm, sweet as a peach, just like Marco said." Heat floods me and I can feel my juices starting to drip down me.

Zo seems to want to take his time and savor this. It's amazing and frustrating at the same time because all I want, no, all I need, is his cock inside me now.

"Please, Zo I need more," I mewl, and he smiles so big, his eyes darkening.

In one quick move my legs are thrown over his shoulders and his face hovers just above my soaking wet center.

"I'm going to make you come, and when I do, I want to hear my name on your lips."

My breathing hitches, and he instantly begins feasting on me.

"Oh God..." I moan, arching my body into him, but he quickly places a hand over my abdomen to hold me down.

His tongue makes intoxicating circles over my clit before he moves down to slide it into my entrance and back again. Beautiful, delicious pleasure builds as he works me with his expert tongue.

My thighs tremble as I near the edge and he slides two figures into me, while circling my clit with his tongue.

"Zo... I am not going to last."

"Good, come for me like a good girl."

I unravel at his words.

"Oh. My. Enzo..." My orgasm crashes through me with such an intensity, I swear I see stars and melt into a boneless bliss.

Zo moves off me and pulls me into his arms. I nestle into him reaching for his pants, but he grabs my hand and stops me.

"Tonight was about you, Sweet Peach. Do you feel better?"

I nod.

"Zo, let me take care of you." I'm still breathless from my orgasm.

"No, now get some sleep."

"Please... I don't want to owe you anything." I protest, but he holds me tighter.

"You never owed me anything before and you don't now. Get some rest, please." He kisses the top of my head. "You need it."

I want to argue more, but the exhaustion is strong and I feel so blissful, and cared for, that sleep threatens to take me before he even finished his sentence.

Snuggling into his arms, I allow him to win this round.

Chapter 7
Nico

The club tonight is bouncing and full of women ripe for the taking. On a normal night, I would find a girl and enjoy a quick fuck in my office to work out this pent-up rage, but the only woman I can think about is Chelsey.

That girl fucking slapped me! I'm thankful the boys were there because I was about to lose my shit. All I wanted to do was show her the man I can really be. I would have taken her to my room, tied her to my bed, and left her there all damn night. I want her to know beyond a doubt that she is mine to do with as I see fit, and if she thinks slapping me will go unpunished, she is greatly mistaken.

I'm sure Enzo is treating her like a princess, but I will do no such thing. She wants to act like a brat, then I will treat her as such.

"Sir, there is a man here requesting an audience with you." Mark's voice fills the walkie earpiece we all wear. My head bouncer is working the door tonight, and I'm thankful for his distraction.

"Does this man have a name?" My voice is clipped and stern. This is who we have to be when we do business. No kindness, no mercy, but I'm sure by now Mark knows the big hearts we have. He has worked for me for close to seven years now.

"David Ryan, sir."

The man who tortures people for his own sick enjoyment, and the man who planned to sell my girl to

Riccardo. A smirk flashes across my face. *This could be incredibly fun.*

"Escort him to my office and let Marco know what's going on."

"Yes sir."

David is the first to enter, Mark and Marco close behind. This isn't the first time we have had a meeting like this, so my boys know their roles. Marco walks to stand next to me as I take a seat. Mark stays at the door to ensure no one leaves or enters without my command.

David takes his seat across from me and I lean back in my chair, looking incredibly disinterested in him. But I couldn't be more interested in why David Ryan is here sitting across from me. He looks a little nervous and he should. I am, after all, his associate's biggest rival.

From the corner of my eye, I see Marco leans against the wall behind me, pinning David with a stare that promises death should he make a wrong move.

Marco may be my goofy, fun loving brother, but he also is quick to anger and acts on it. I don't doubt the earlier suspicions of Chelsey's past still play in his mind. I just hope he doesn't do anything stupid.

"So David. You mind telling me why exactly you're here?" I keep my voice monotone.

"Yes, I'm here to request your permission to spend some time in Seattle. I don't want issues with me being here, but I got word that my daughter Chelsey is somewhere around here."

I raise an eyebrow at him and lean forward on my desk.

"So you want to conduct a manhunt in my territory and you're here for what? My blessing?" My voice sharpens as I pin him with a cold stare.

"I'm here for my daughter and I don't want trouble, just safe passage."

"Hmm, well all I see is one of Riccardo's dogs sniffing around and gathering intel." I lean back. "I've heard nothing of your daughter being here. So give me one good reason not to have my brother here kill you."

David squirms and I have to suppress my smile. Marco takes his queue and pushes off the wall with a cold grin before pulling out a large knife from beneath my desk.

"Shit," David mumbles and shifts uncomfortably in his seat. "I really am just looking for my daughter." His eyes are locked on Marco, a bead of sweat rolling off his forehead. "I get why you wouldn't want me in your territory, but I'm not going to just leave her active trail here. You can understand that right?"

"What I don't understand David, is why you want her back so badly?" I stand and lean on the desk toward him. "We all know you used her as a drug runner. Are you that desperate for workers?"

"How dare you patronize me and imply I don't care for my daughter Nico!" He stands, planting his hands on the desk in front of me. Poor fucker doesn't even realize the mistake he has just made.

Marco moves at lightning speed, stabbing the knife right through his hand and into the cedar wood of my desk.

David cries out in agony and bends at the knees, wanting to collapse.

"Look at me you worthless bastard," Marco commands, and David slowly pulls his eyes from the knife in his hand to look at my brother. "You will treat my brother with respect, and you will only address him as Mr. Romano." Marco growls ripping the knife out of his hand.

"Escort David out of the club." I tilt my head to Mark in the corner before turning back to the miserable fuck in front of me. "And David, If I catch you in my city, you will lose that hand. So make sure you leave town quickly. My brother here would love nothing more than to handle getting rid of you for me."

David is reluctant, but Mark drags him out and I'm thankful the trash is gone.

"How did he find out Chelsey is here in Seattle?" Marco slams his fist down on my desk in front of me, anger radiating off him. "The girl was damn near impossible to track down."

Anger pulses through me, but I have more to think about. My biggest concern is if David goes to Riccardo with this information.

"Calm down. Chelsey is safe at the apartment with Enzo."

"I know, but because you denied him, he may go to Riccardo and then we will have bigger problems." He groans, dragging a hand over his face.

I'm not prepared to go to war with Riccardo over her, but I also won't allow him to dig around my territory or force my hand.

"Riccardo won't set foot in our city without concrete intel and neither him nor David have that." I try to reassure him. It's all true, but that doesn't stop the anxiety forming in my chest.

"Fine, but at least text Enzo about what happened," he barks as he leaves my office.

I wish I had the luxury of feeling all my emotions, but when I get emotional people die. And if war is brewing, I cannot allow my emotions to cloud my judgment. My brothers are my only family left, they are the most important thing to me, and I will *not* let anything happen to them.

Chapter 8

Chelsey

The sun shines through my bedroom window, waking me earlier than I would like. I've been here almost a full month now and today is a rare day of waking up alone. Every night I spent with either Marco or Enzo, and that usually ends up with us having sex and then snuggling for the night.

I climb from my bed and throw on my V-neck red t-shirt and cotton shorts. It's Sunday, which means the guys were at the club late. Here and there, they have started leaving me with their security guys, Mitch or Mark, when they're all needed for the evening. Last night was one of them. I creep down the hallway towards the kitchen, and the house is silent. The guys must still be sleeping, and Mitch is gone from his spot in the hall. Anticipation and adrenalin fill me. This is the first opportunity I've had to look for a way out. One of the guys almost always has eyes on me, and when they don't, they are still close enough to hear me.

And while I've enjoyed the sex and security, and my time with Zo and Marco. But I'm still just a prisoner. Still not free to come and go as I please.

The elevator is out, it has a thumbprint scanner and a code box. And the doors never open without one or the other. But maybe the code is in Nico's office...

I move through the house once more, listening for any indication that the guys might be stirring, but nothing. The office door is shut and I wouldn't put it past Nico to have it locked. He has made it clear how much he doesn't trust me and never fails to show his complete disdain for my presence.

But I've got to try. I push the handle down and it gives. Blowing out a breath of relief, I open the door to his desk in the corner with filing cabinets on the far wall. Curiosity pricks at my mind as I take in the full size couch on the wall opposite his desk. What on earth could he use that for?

I pull my attention back to the task at hand and move quickly to his desk. Random papers are thrown about among random sticky notes everywhere. For a controlling asshole you'd think he would be more organized, but the fact that he isn't might just be to my benefit.

Shuffling through the finances, receipts, I find really nothing of substance. It's probably a lost cause. I sigh in frustration and sit down in his oversized computer chair, a yellow sticky note just barely peeking out from a drawer catching my eye. My stomach swirls a little with hope that this is my ticket to freedom, but there is also a strange feeling there too. One I won't be addressing right now.

I try to open the drawer, but it's locked. Reaching a cross the desk, I grab two paper clips out of the small dish. I bend and shape them how I need to pick the lock. Twisting and bending them with precision until the lock gives way. *Gotcha.*

Pulling the drawer open, I grab the edge of note and Five numbers stare me in the face. It's not labeled, but worth a try. I leave his office in a hurry, not bothering to close the door. Nothing else matters except getting to that elevator and getting the hell out of here!

Arriving in front of the big metal door, I open the code panel and punch in the numbers. I'm ready to vomit and jittery with anxiety. This needs to work. The words accepted pop up on the screen and relief hits me as the doors open.

Stepping inside, I close my eyes. *This is it, I'm free.* I'll get out of here and steal some shoes, then find Slim and hit the road to Arizona.

I stand in the silence, waiting for the doors to close and that weird feeling comes back once more. My brain wonders to Enzo to Marco... No more movie nights, cooking in the kitchen, or sexy games.

I... I'm going to miss them. My chest aches slightly at the realization I will never see them again.

A hand slams between the closing metal doors, and my eyes jolt open. The doors open to reveal Nico sporting his gray sweatpants and a look of pure outrage.

"What the fuck are you doing?" he growls and I gulp. His eyes scan over me, landing on the yellow sticky note clutched in my hand. He cocks his head and pins me with his eyes as he steps into the elevator. I don't dare move. He smacks the ground level button behind him, his eyes never leaving mine. The door closes and we head toward the ground, while my heart rate spikes.

"What are you doing?" I ask, fear starting to fill my chest. He's going to put me in a body bag for this one.

"This was your big plan huh? Sneak into my office, then run out of here half dressed, with no shoes?" He steps more into my space and I step back until I hit the wall. "For a woman who survived David for a father, who managed to evade people looking for her for months, this is a pretty stupid plan." His words are acid and I want to shy away, but I won't.

The doors ding open and he steps aside, giving me a clear path to run. This isn't right. I shake my head, pressing myself to the wall harder.

"What you're just letting me go?" I ask in apprehension.

"Yeah, you want to leave so damn bad. Then go." He throws his hand out, pointing for me to leave. "Go take your chance in this city with your dad knowing you're in Seattle."

My eyes turn to saucers and my breath leaves my lungs. "What? How do you know my dad knows I'm here?"

Nico moves to step in front of me, his voice threateningly low. "Because he came to see me last month and my brothers and I fucking protected your ass!"

All the fight leaves me. *They protected me...*

"Now make your choice. You are either ours and we will protect you as such, or you fucking leave and never come back," he hisses, stepping aside once more.

The choice is obvious. If my dad and Riccardo know I'm here, I'll never escape without being caught. I'm good, but not that good. "I'll stay." My voice is meek and I drop my eyes to stare at the floor.

Nico doesn't say a word, turning around to face the door. He hits the button for the apartment and places his thumb on the scanner.

The elevator ride is slow and heavy as I reconcile myself with my choice. Even if it wasn't really a choice. There will be no escape plan now. I'm at their mercy.

The doors open to the apartment and Nico storms out without bothering to look back at me. Tears fill my eyes, silently streaming down my face.

What do I do now? How do I move forward?

I take a step and another until I'm back in my room. Flopping down on the bed, I cry until there is nothing left.

This is it.

It's over.

All hope for a different future gone.

I'm not sure how long I've laid here for, but a knock sounds on my door.

"Please go away," I yell as I wrap myself around my pillow.

Whoever it is doesn't listen, because my door creaks open. A large body flops on to the bed beside me and I don't bother looking, I can tell it's Marco as the smell of his shampoo fills my nose.

"Why are you hiding out in here?" he asks, wrapping an arm around my torso.

"Not right now, Marco. My brain is too full," I mumble into the pillow.

"Did you not sleep well or something?" His confusion fills his voice as he moves a hair from my face.

"I slept fine," I snap, releasing the pillow and rolling to face him fully. "Why didn't you tell me my dad went to see Nic?"

His eyebrows shoot up and his head slides back slightly. "How do you know about that, Little Bird?"

"Nic told me this morning!" I sit up to climb off the bed. "I could have ended up in Riccardo's filthy hands!"

He moves to my side and grips my face in his hands. "We would've never let that happen."

"I tried to run away this morning! I almost played right into his hand because I didn't know the truth."

His brows furrow and he takes a step back.

"You were going to leave without evening saying good bye?" Hurt registers over his features. "I know we brought you here by force, and Nic has been nothing but a rude ass."

He pauses and wet his lips. "But I thought we were forming something good here…"

My chest pangs at his look of betrayal. He's right. We do have something good going here. We have been fuck buddies, friends even. I didn't think about how me leaving might hurt them too.

"Yeah. I was, and I didn't think about how it would hurt you and Enzo. I'm sorry." I step forward, taking his hand in mine. "But I'm here now and won't be leaving. I have to stay. Can we just pretend all of this never happened?"

His eyes search mine for a moment before a small smirk forms on his lips. "Fine, but it will cost you making lunch. I'm thinking BLTs with fries," he teases and I smack him in the chest.

"Fine. BLTs to buy your forgiveness." I roll my eyes and head to the kitchen, Marco chuckling behind me.

Chapter 9

Enzo

C helsey saunters into the kitchen, and my chest instantly warms. I've grown a bit attached over the past month, but that's something I keep to myself. Nic would just lecture me on how she's temporary Marco would say I'm being a dumb ass, and she wouldn't reciprocate.

"Hey there Sweet Peach." I turn, leaning my back to the counter to watch as she pulls things from the fridge. "I was going to wake you up this morning, but Nic said not too and then I lost the rock, paper, scissors match with Marco."

"It's all good." She shrugs, not moving from her task. *That's her only response?* Normally she is more talkative and chipper. She moves to the stove and lays some bacon out in a pan.

Walking behind her, I place a hand on each of her hips.

"Are you okay?" I ask with concern.

"Fine. Just making some lunch," she says without turning to face me. Something is wrong here.

"Did Marco or Nic do something to-"

She whirls around to face me with a scowl.

"No, I'm fine!" she scoffs and turns back to the bacon. "I just have a lot on my mind."

"Oh, okay. Anything I can help with?"

"Yeah. Cut the tomato slices please." She gestures to the other items on the counter. That's not what I meant, and she knows it, but I take the hint. If it were something big, I would have been informed by now.

We work in silence, the only sounds are my knife hitting the cutting board and the bacon sizzling in the pan. It's odd for us to be completely silent, but I appreciate her presence none the less. After the bacon is cooked, I start assembling sandwiches while she moves through the kitchen like this is her own home and I love the domestic feel of it. She opens the oven door to throw in a tray of fries and I turn back to the next sandwich to build.

"Fuck! Damn it!" she yells slamming the oven door.

Dropping the bread, I walk to her as she inspects her arm.

"Come here." I take hold of her and begin doing my own inspection. "Are you okay?" There is a red welt forming on her forearm that may bubble into a second-degree burn. "Did you get burned anywhere else?"

"I'm fine. It's just a burn." She tries to pull her arm away, but I don't let her. I wrap my arm around her waist and walk her to the sink, placing the burn under the cool water.

"This could blister. It needs to be taken care of." She shakes her head as if it's nothing. "MARCO!"

Nic enters the kitchen a second later and walks straight to us. "What happened?"

"Nothing. It's -"

"She burned herself on the oven. I was calling for Marco so he could get the burn cream out of the first aid kit."

Nic's eyebrows furrow as he looks at her arm and then at her. She drops her face, not looking at him. Did something happen that I don't know about? Now is not the time to ask, but I will later.

Marco jogs into the kitchen and rushes to us all huddled at the sink.

"What happened? Are you okay, Little Bird?"

"For the love of all that is good in the world. I. Am. Fine." She pulls her arm from the water and tries to walk away, but Nico grabs her, taking hold of her arm to look at closer.

"She burned herself. Marco, go get the burn cream," he orders and Marco takes off. He turns his gaze to Chelsey and his face softens. "Fine or not, this needs to be taken care of or it could get infected." His voice is smooth like whiskey. It's the same way he would talk to Marco and I as kids when we messed up.

Nic rarely softens his dominating asshole demeanor, but for some reason, Chelsey brings it out in him and it's refreshing to see.

Marco returns with the cream and I take the bottle from him. I take her arm from Nic and begin applying the smooth white substance and her tension leaves her shoulders.

When I'm done, her gaze meets mine and a soft smile spreads her lips, her eyes alight with a deep a emotion that I can't read. Care maybe, but whatever it is, it's something more than the surface level she has been showing us since we brought her here.

"Thank you for taking care of me," she says softly, and her eyes bounce over each of my brothers. "I really do appreciate you and what we have here."

A longing to kiss her pulls at me, and I hope my brothers feel it too. We sit in this silent vulnerability for a long moment before she pulls her arm away and takes a step back from us. I can damn near see the wall she is putting back in place.

"Well besides the fries, lunch is done. I... Uh... I need to go check on something." She jogs out of the kitchen and the soft moment is gone.

My chest pangs for a second after she disappeared, but I ignore it. Nic's hard demeanor returns as he stuffs his hands in his pockets and squares his shoulders.

"I need to head to the club and Marco, you need to come with me. Mitch found someone messing with Mrs. Hotch's girls on the avenue."

"Did anyone get hurt?" Concern laces my voice. Mrs. Hotch is a nice lady and makes sure the working girls don't get hurt by johns.

"Everyone is fine." Nic moves to the elevator and Marco grabs a sandwich, then joins him grinning ear to ear. *Sadistic fuck.*

I watch them enter the elevator and head off to do the task I hate the most. The timer goes off for the fries reminding me my Sweet Peach left without lunch.

Pulling them from the oven, I quickly make a small plate for her, then start toward her room. I hope she welcomes the company. She has been out of sorts all afternoon, and I want to know why.

I knock lightly on the door, and she doesn't respond. "Chelsey?" I call out as I enter. She isn't in here.

I set her plate down on her dresser and begin my hunt.

First the small library- Nope.

I move to the gym- Nope.

My heart pounds in my chest. Where the hell could she have gone? I run around the apartment, checking every room I can think of. Did she leave? My stomach sinks at the idea she could be gone for good. To never hear her laugh, or feel her soft skin again.

I run to the storage room next to Nic's office, hoping she is hiding in there. It's a stupid notion, but I have to be sure. I get to the door and swing it wide. She's not in here, but the door to the roof is ajar. She has to be on the roof.

I climb the stairs, praying I'm right. There isn't much up here except a small patio set so we can eat outside during the summer.

I slide the final door open and she's sitting in a chair with her knees tucked to her chest, basking in the new summer rays. Relief washes over me at the sight of her.

"I thought you bailed on me," I tease, masking my relief with humor.

She startles, dropping her legs to the ground, a hand flying to her chest.

"Jesus, Enzo. You scared me."

I walk over and take a seat next to her.

"I didn't mean to. How'd you know there was stuff up here?"

"Marco showed me last week." She brushes her hair from her face and smiles at me. "It's become a good place for me to clear my head."

I lean forward and take her hand in mine. "I'm glad. Anything you want to talk about? You were a little out of sorts earlier."

She adjusts in her chair to sit straighter and my stomach sours. She is going to talk to me about something serious, or at least I think she is. It won't be an easy conversation, because people don't move when they tell you they hate tomatoes.

"I can't leave," she says softly, and I lean forward, my eyebrows pinched together in confusion.

"I know, we took you and you live with us until we say otherwise." It tastes sour coming out of my mouth, but that's the blunt truth. She is still our little hostage.

"No, Zo. I had an opportunity to leave today. Nic even said he'd let me go."

I release her hand and sit back in my seat. I'm not sure what hurts worse, the fact that I almost lost her and never even knew, or that my brother was going to allow it without even bothering to talk to me.

"But I can't leave. My dad knows I'm in Seattle. I have to stay." She pauses and I want to explode. I want to hurt her like she is hurting me. I mean nothing to her...

"But Zo, when I got on that elevator. I realized I was going to miss you and Marco, and that fact is just as hard to wrap my brain around." It comes out almost as soft as a whisper and she shakes her head, like she can shake the feeling off.

She cares...

My chest fills with warmth at her confession. She was still willing to leave us behind, but on some level, she cares about us. I stand, offering her my hand, and she takes it to stand next to me.

"That's enough talking. I think the problem is, you're in your head to much."

She pinches her eyebrows and eyes me curiously.

"We are going to remedy that." I scoop her up and throw her over my shoulder.

"Zo," she squeals, and I smack her ass. "What are you doing?" "Taking you to get out of your head and maybe a little dirty." I walk over to the access door and swing it wide, marching us down until we are back in the apartment.

"Any objections to this plan?" I ask, leaving the storage room.

"None whatsoever." She giggles and I can only picture how red her sweet little cheeks are.

Back in the kitchen, I plop her butt down on to the counter and move to the fridge.

"What are you doing?" she asks giggling again and the sound lights a fire in me. I haven't even revealed my plan, and it's already working.

I grab the pint of peanut butter ice cream, then pull out two spoons, then finally, Marco's new package of Oreos.

With everything in hand, I turn to her. "Stay on that counter Sweet Peach, or there will be hell to pay," I tease, and she giggles some more.

I take everything to the living room and place it on the coffee table. Jogging back, I find she is right where I left her with the sweetest damn smile.

Taking hold of her, I throw her over my shoulder once more.

"Zo!" she squeals. "I can walk you know."

"Not a chance." I toss her on the couch and she bounces, releasing another laugh.

"Alright, pick your emotional food." I gesture to the sweets. "Ice cream, Oreos, or both."

"Of course both!"

I wink at her, grabbing the snacks and spoons. Then sit on the couch across from her and set the items between us.

She grabs the Oreos, as I rip the top open on the ice cream.

We sit there laughing and making small talk until the ice cream is gone and the Oreos are half gone. This is what she needed. To feel normal for a while and stop stressing. Is her life fucked up, absolutely, but now she has us to help her bear the weight of it. She just has to trust us enough.

The elevator digs and Nic strolls past the living room in different clothes, not even bothering to say hello, Marco following close behind. Things must have gotten messy, because it looks like they both showered at the club.

Marco smiles as soon as he sees her and I know he is getting attached like I am. He walks around the couch then scowls.

"Really, my cookies again?" He huffs without an ounce of actual anger in his voice.

Chelsey shrugs. "We needed comfort food."

He shakes his head in fake indignation. Then kisses the top of her head and sits on the floor next to her.

"And did it help?" She nods with a beautiful smile as she stuffs another cookie in her mouth. God, she is so damn cute, even with cookie crumbs all over her face.

"How's the burn?"

Shit, I never even thought to check on that again.

"Fine." She shrugs again.

"Let me see."

She huffs and rolls her eyes before extending her arm. It welted and has a white inflamed bubble on it.

"Shit, this probably needs to see the doctor," he mumbles.

"I agree," I say more firmly than he did.

She pulls her arm away and looks at herself. "It's not that bad. I've had worse."

Marco and I stare at her, urging her silently to explain.

"You know the scar on my back." She pauses, taking a deep breath. "That was a burn. A bad one and I never saw a doctor for it." That explains why it wasn't in any of her records. Marco leans forward and takes her hand.

"My dad gave it to me when I didn't do as I was told shortly after my eighteenth birthday."

Anger threatens to boil out of me at the confession. But she shared that with us. If I go off now, she might not trust me to share anymore.

What kind of monster inflicts that type of wound on their own child. One day David Ryan will get what's coming to him and for once, that will be a death I will enjoy having a hand in.

Marco closes his eyes, taking deep breaths, and Chelsey watches him with wide eyes. My brother is a hot head, but he cannot handle this wrong. Not after today…

"I'm sorry that happened to you, but thank you for telling us about it." I lean forward to kiss her. Nothing I said wasn't true, but my brother need a minute to compose himself.

"Yeah, Little Bird. You're a fucking warrior," he says standing to kiss her too. "But you still need a doctor for that arm."

"Fine, but if you're going to call in a doctor anyway. I need my next birth control shot too," she says, her cheeks turning pink as she bites her bottom lip. I smile at her shyness and nervous energy.

"We can do that. I'm not ready for babies anytime soon," Marco teases as Nic reappears from the hallway.

"Marco. Get changed. We leave for work in twenty," Nic commands, adjusting his watch.

"Enjoy your night and please don't eat all of my cookies," Marco teases before kissing the top of her head

"No promises," she yells at him before he shakes his head and disappears down the hall.

Her attention turns back to me and I want to address something before too much time passes.

"You know there is no need to be nervous or embarrassed to tell us your needs." I smile, hoping to reassure her.

"Thank you, but telling you isn't what makes me nervous. I just don't like doctors." She says it like it's no big deal, and I know she's holding back, but I won't press.

Tonight is my night off, and I didn't get my Sweet Peach last night, so I want to enjoy her now that her sweet ass is mine until dawn.

• • • ● ● • ● ● ● • •

I startle awake by a bang in the hall.

"Aw fuck!" Marco quietly yells and I turn to check and make sure my Sweet Peach is still asleep.

Sliding my arm from beneath her, I gently roll off the bed and slide on my sweatpants before going to check on my brother.

Opening the door, I find Marco in the hallway rubbing his hand next to a large hole in the wall.

"What happened?" I ask raising an eyebrow.

"I wasn't paying attention and tripped over my own feet. When I fell, I put my hand through the damn wall." He sounds completely annoyed and Nic will be too when he sees it.

I move from the door frame and look at his hand. He's lucky he only has a red mark. Nothing got split open or cut.

"Please tell me how you can punch a wall with no damage, but our girl can't even put fries in the oven without needing a doctor," I tease, and a smirk forms on his face.

"Talent little brother." He smirks, then drops his hands to the side. "She still doing okay?"

"Yeah, but now that I know you're not dying, I'm going to go back to her."

He snickers and waves his hand.

I turn and head back to into her room, but she has moved from this small ball on the side to a total star fish in the middle. I sit on the edge of her bed, simply to admire her, and I can't bring myself to disturb her. I guess the rest of my night will be spent in my cold bed.

Chapter 10
Chelsey

I'm jolted from my nightmare by strong arms wrapping around me. My mother dropping dead in front of me still fresh in my mind

"Shhh, you're safe." Nico's smooth voice soothes my trembling body. "I've got you."

I turn into him, desperate for comfort, any comfort. He holds me silently, stroking my back, while I put my pieces back together.

"I get nightmares too sometimes," he says and confusion fills me. Why is he here and what could this mountain of man possibly have nightmares about? I pull back to look at him but he pulls me back so I can't.

"My parents were murdered when I was nineteen." His confession hits me square in the chest, but I don't say anything. "I got into a fight with the heir to the Mexican Cartel and ended up killing him. I was angry and hurt about him fucking my girlfriend. That night his father and men came into our hotel room. He killed my parents, then told me that my greatest penance would be living with what I caused." My heart aches for him and I grip him tighter. "He was right. All these years later, I still have nightmares about it."

Nico stands from the bed, and I watch him adjust his tee shirt. "We all fight battles Chelsey, it's just nice to not have to always fight them alone," he says and then sucks in a breath. "I couldn't listen to you suffering alone tonight, but please don't tell my brothers about what I told you."

"I won't," I promise and sit up, clutching my blanket to my chest. He nods and then leaves.

• • • ● ● • ● ● • • •

"Good morning, Little Bird," Macro coos and my eyes flutter open. A smile spreads across my face as he stares at me, leaning on his elbow.

"Good morning," I say with a yawn, taking in his sweet smile. "Don't get me wrong, I'm happy to see you, but I recall going to bed with Zo last night." And waking up to Nico...

He knits his brows together, but it's quickly replaced with his playful charm.

"Well, Enzo needed to talk with Nic this morning, so I figured I would join you here." He winks at me seductively and memories of the last time we were in my bed together flood my brain. Heat fills my core and I bite my lower lip.

"Oh, well thank you I guess. I would have hated to get cold this morning." My breathing shallows.

Really, you couldn't come up with a better response! Come on stupid brain work!

Marco gives me a crooked smile, and his eyes darken. I seem to be doing terribly at hiding my desire.

"Well I'm here to serve. Now are there any other needs I can assist with?" His voice is low and seductive.

I'm biting my lip so hard, I worry it may bleed when I release it. But I shake my head, forcefully, unable to speak because the only words I want to utter are 'fuck me Marco.' *God, I need boundaries.*

Yesterday was way more emotional than it should have been, especially last night, and having sex with these guys over and over isn't going to make those emotions go away! I'd love it if my body could get the memo though, because these guys have turned me into a horny sex monster.

"No? Okay, well, I can leave you alone then," he says as he sits up and moves off of the bed.

Before I even think about it, I grab his arm. "Wait!" I half shout at him.

"What for? If you have no other needs." He's playing with me now, knowing how much my traitorous body wants him.

Marco slides back into bed, and my body feels like it's humming at his touch.

"Marco please..."

"Oh no, Little Bird. I need to hear you say the words." His voice, smooth and tormenting, sends shivers through me. "Now, what do you need?"

I stare at his perfect form for a long minute, allowing my eyes to rake over his shirtless body and already tented gray sweatpants. He wants this too.

Shifting to reach him better, I trace my fingers over his chest. He sucks in a breath, and I slide my fingers down his hard muscles and warm skin. Marco's lustful gaze never leaves mine. Reaching the waistband of his pants, he quickly grabs my wrist.

"That's cheating," he growls darkly. "I said to use your words. Now, what do you want?" His voice is deep and husky, and I damn near moan at the sound of it. This is becoming torture.

"Marco..." My cheeks heat at the words about to leave my lips. "Would you fuck me. Please."

He smiles like he has just won a gold medal at the Olympics or something. And in one quick motion, he is on top of me, claiming me with a deep kiss.

His hand caresses my body and I arch into his touch, moaning into his lips.

How are these men so intoxicating?

He sits up, ripping open my shirt, and a gasp escapes me at the suddenness. He wastes no time removing my shorts, leaving me bare before him.

The onslaught of attention he is giving me has my sex throbbing.

Within a second, he flips me onto my stomach, pulling me onto my hands and knees by my waist.

"Last time I went easy on you, but now I'm going to give it all to you. You ready for that?"

I moan my reply with a nod.

"Words now Little Bird."

"Yes," I breathe, my heartbeat racing. "Fuck me please." I press my backside against him, his cock twitching against me.

This man is going to be the death of me if he doesn't fuck me soon!

Fingers run through my slick folds and he groans. "So fucking wet for me all ready"

This is it, this is how I die. Chelsey Ryan, death by sexual denial.

He slides two fingers into my entrance. My body arches against them, begging for more. His free hand finds my breast, teasing my nipple, sending a shiver through me.

His fingers pump in and out of me with steady rhythm, and I thrust against them, fucking his fingers relentlessly.

"I see you got the fun started without me." Zo's voice pulls my attention, and I look over to see him standing in the doorway, his gaze dark and full of desire, palming himself through his gray sweatpants.

I may burst into flames with the level of heat I feel. I extend my hand, reaching for him, meeting his gaze.

His eyebrows raise. "You want me to join you, Sweet Peach?"

Nodding, I moan through the pleasure Marco continues to give my pussy.

"We are using our words today," Marco commands, smacking my ass hard.

The pain of the spanking sends me over the edge. My climax peaks with a crushing wave, and I cry out.

Marco doesn't stop. Working me relentlessly, drawing out my orgasm.

"Do you want Enzo to join us, Little Bird?"

"Yes" I breathe out.

Zo wastes no time and is naked and next to me in less than a minute. "Come here, Sweet Peach."

I climb on top of him, reveling in his soft kisses and in his soft hands trailing over my ribs up to my breasts.

Marco relaxes next to us, stroking himself, smirking, daring me. Fuck... I want that job.

Zo holds me close as I reach over and grab Marco's large, firm cock, stroking it with the perfect amount of pressure. He hisses at my touch, watching me swipe my thumb through his pre-cum.

"Oh fuck. That's perfect, Little Bird," he groans.

"Why don't you come sit on my face while working my brother?"

Fuck yes...

I do as I am told, hovering my aching pussy over Zo's face, but he pulls me down, beginning his beautiful torture. His mouth sucks and nips my clit, making light circles with his tongue. He drives me higher and higher, and it takes everything I have not to collapse. But the moans escaping his throat tell me he wouldn't mind.

"Oh God..." I mewl, my eyes falling shut as I give myself over to them.

Beautiful pleasure builds and builds. When I'm on the edge of oblivion once again Zo stops, moving me off his face.

"What no! Please..."

Marco flashes me a wicked smile and sits up.

He drags my backside down to him, pressing a finger on my dark hole.

"Have you ever been fucked here?"

I shake my head no, lost in the pleasure. Marco spanks me again, hard, and I cry out, but wetness floods my center.

"Words," he commands, and it's so damn sexy.

"No."

"Okay, I'll be gentle."

My breathing hitches as butterflies fill me with the nerves of what is about to happen.

"Me first though." Zo enters my pussy slowly.

Moaning at the intrusion of his thick long cock, I revel in the sensation. The fullness of him is maddening. He pumps in and out of me at a slow teasing pace.

"Fuck... Your pussy is perfect, Sweet Peach," he groans, throwing his head back, enjoying his own pleasure.

I hear Marco squirt something that I only assume is lube and my body tenses.

Zo stills inside me, pulling my face to his chest, and I feel Marco's hand on my ass.

"We got you Chelsey. You still want this?" Zo's voice soothes as my breathing picks up and my body tenses.

I have done a lot with men, but fucking two at the same time is not one.

My brain is screaming at me to stop this. But my body is singing for them.

"Yes," I breathe.

Zo wraps his arms around me, stilling me as Marco's head press against me.

"Relax, Little Bird. You got to let me in," Marco soothes as he rubs a hand over my ass.

I do my best to relax, allowing him to enter.

"Oh God!" I bellow at the burning pain, feeling myself stretch to accommodate him.

"Shh, almost there. You're taking me so well." His praise stokes the fire in me and once he is fully seated they both remain still, allowing me to adjust to them.

"Are you okay?" Zo asks, stroking a stray tear from my face.

"Yes." I can feel my body relax.

"Good girl. Now just stay still and allow us to do the work," Marco says, kissing my back.

They both begin to move and the burning quickly gives way to pleasure. Beautiful pressure builds in my core like never before.

"Oh, fuck!" I bellow at their onslaught.

The fullness of them has my thighs quaking and my walls fluttering around them.

"I'm not going to... Ahhh!" A strong, amazing orgasm crashes through me, and I damn near see stars at the intensity of it!

"Oh Shit Chelsey!" Marco barks as he spills into me, quickly followed by Zo's grunt and him filling my pussy.

Boneless, I am utterly boneless. The boys slide out of me, then sandwich me between them.

We lay in bed together, each of us enjoy our post fuck bliss.

My ass throbs from what just occurred, but that was the best sex I have ever had. The fullness, the intensity, the pain and the pleasure. It all combined to create an earth-shattering level orgasm.

If it was this good with both of them, how good might it be with all three of them...

Stop now! Nico is an ass-hat and you don't want him, even if he shows you his soft side here and there. But what if I kind of do?

"Let's get you cleaned up." Zo picks me up off the bed, taking me to the bathroom, Marco walking close behind. My body is drained, but my heart for once is full from how much they care for me.

Chapter 11
Marco

Enzo has always been the caretaker. Personally, I've never had a desire to care for a woman after sex. I figure it's their job. Chelsey is not just another woman though. She's my woman, and boy does she surprise me at every turn.

She is nothing like I thought she would be. She seems to enjoy fucking us, as much as we enjoy fucking her, and is willing to trust us with her body completely. I have had plenty of great women in bed before, but none compare to her.

Enzo cradles her to his chest, standing in the corner, while I draw her a warm bath with Epsom salt to sooth her thoroughly spanked cheeks and fucked ass.

I loved seeing her ass cherry red from my hand, and if that damn river between her thighs was any indication, she enjoyed it as much as I did. The memory of that is going to be imprinted on my brain for life, and damn if my cock isn't already getting hard just thinking about it.

The bath is drawn and Enzo lowers her into it. She lets out the sweetest of pleasure filled moans as her body relaxes into the water. My heart swells a little at the sight. Is this why he takes care of his women? For this warm and fuzzy type feeling? It's a nice, but uncomfortable feeling.

I'm totally fucked when it comes to this woman. I quickly climb into the tub, pulling her into my chest. She responds instantly by cuddling into me.

I have never done this with someone before, but it was a need inside me to hold her, to stroke her hair, to feel her warmth.

Enzo pins me with his eyes and it's probably because I stole his spot in this tub with her, but I don't care. He got the bottom with her, and then got the snuggles while I got the bath ready. This is my time now.

"Marco." Chelsey's soft, tired voice vibrates against my chest.

"Yes, Little Bird?" I coo back, moving her silk soft hair from her face.

"Why do you call me Little Bird?" She shifts to look at me.

My eyes search hers and they twinkle like a star in the night sky, and there's a glow of contentment about her.

"Because you flew away from your nest. You could have fallen to your death, but you learned to fly and you were strong enough to stay away from the predators. The name Little Bird is meant for your strength." I brush my thumb along her cheek, and she graces me with a soft smile then reaches up, kissing me softly.

The kiss isn't like the lust and desired filled kisses we have shared, but something deeper. I have never allowed myself to have strong feelings for a woman, but this woman is breaking down my walls whether I want her to or not. I don't think I'm ever going to be able to let her go without killing a piece of me.

She breaks the kiss and cuddles back into my chest, her eyes fluttering closed.

This should be weird, taking a bath with the woman with my brother sitting next to us, but it isn't. It simply feels right. There is no serious jealousy, only contentment.

Enzo stares at her with the same longing I feel towards her, and now we need to figure out how to get our dick-head brother in on this too. She is perfect, and he is too stubborn to see it. He needs to give her a chance, but I don't know if he ever will. Well, not without a push anyway.

Chelsey is damn near passed out on my chest, so Enzo helps her out of the tub and makes his way to the bed.

Dr. Carter is set to come give her burn a look over and administer her birth control shot this afternoon. I think a mention to our older brother about her being nervous will have him hovering over her like a guard dog. Nic isn't a gentle caretaker like Enzo, but he is more protective than the secret service is of the president.

Dr. Carter has been the Romano family doctor for years now, but after we decided Chelsey needed to see a doctor, I'm pretty sure Nic called her at least five times making sure everything was in order.

This should be just the thing to get him more involved, but only the Lord above can keep his asshole side at bay. If that comes out again, I'm not sure what our girl will do, because she isn't scared of him.

"Enzo, are you good with her? I need to talk to Nic."

"More than good. Go and let me enjoy our woman all to myself."

I roll my eyes as he wraps her into his chest.

Dressed, I make my way to Nic's office. He practically lives in there with how much he works.

Entering, he doesn't even bother to look up from his computer screen. The tension is heavy and I swear if he doesn't release some of it soon, he is going to have a heart attack.

"So I was just with Chels-"

"Of course you were. It's where you and Enzo always are. This girl is really getting to be more trouble than she is worth!" he booms.

"Seriously, Nic! You've hardly given her a chance!" I level him with my stare. "I only came here to tell you that she's really fuckin nervous about Dr. Carter this afternoon. So get over your shit!" I yell then storm out of his office.

He's wound so fucking tight he doesn't even realize he's strangling himself and I swear if he screws things up with our girl, I will lose it on him. He may be the oldest, but that doesn't make him lord of all.

I make my way to our gym to burn off this new found anger I have towards my brother at the moment. Running on the treadmill usually does the trick and that better be the fucking case today or I may smack Nic on the side of the head with a frying pan and give Dr. Carter something else to look at.

Five miles into my run, someone turns down the blaring rock music.

Instantly my anger returns, apparently I need five more miles. I gear up to lay into whichever brother it was, but when I turn around, Chelsey is leaning against the wall next to the radio in one of my shirts and nothing else. *Is she missing her panties too?*

My anger dissipates immediately, like her presence alone was a bucket of water on my burning fire.

She is my woman, but her wearing my shirt is like she is saying she knows she's mine and nothing has ever been so sexy.

"I'm sorry to interrupt, I just heard the music and then saw you running... Well anyway, I hope it's okay I borrowed one of your shirts?" She looks at me with an awkward glance.

I love how strong she can be, but when she is at ease, she is really kind of shy and it's adorable.

"Oh it's more than alright for you to take one of my shirts." I stop and move of the treadmill. "How about you come here so I can have a better look at you in it?"

Her breathing hitches and my good girl instantly starts walking towards me. Seriously, how could she be any more perfect? If I fuck her in this gym, that counts as another five-mile run right? Yeah I think I am going to count that as the remainder of my work out, because my cock is becoming stiff as iron.

Standing directly in front of me, she eyes my muscular body like she wants me just as bad as I want her.

"Little Bird, were you not satisfied earlier?" I want to be buried in this woman in the next thirty seconds, but playing with her makes fucking her all the sweeter.

"I was.... I just want more." Her voice is completely breathless as she presses her body to mine, gripping the waistband of my sweats.

"Oh well I'm happy to help you with that." My voice is raspy from how much I'm dying to claim her.

She moves before I do, taking complete charge as she slams her lips into mine, and fuck me is it hot. She parts her lips and my tongue invades, tasting her delicious flavor of mint and cherries, and my cock weeps.

A pleasure filled moan escapes her and it's kindling to the fire already burning in me.

Her fingers find my cock and I buck into her hand a little, as she smiles against my lips. She is toying with me just like I did to her earlier. The problem is I'm the master of the game. I am a patient man, I will toy with her until she is begging me for my cock.

Peeling my shirt off of her, I begin kissing her in all the right spots. Working my way down her neck to her beautiful breasts, until I find her nipple and suck it into my mouth.

Her hand flies to my hair, and she throws her head back. "Oh... My... Marco..." she pants and I know I'm already winning at the game we seem to be playing.

"SERIOUSLY!" Nic's voice booms, pulling us from our lust filled haze. "We have a bunch of rooms in this house and you two are trying to fuck in the gym that has a huge glass door, that anyone in the apartment could see into!" He stalks closer, but stops half way to us. "Marco, if anyone besides us saw her naked I would have to kill them, so keep your fucking escapades in the bedroom!"

Chelsey starts shrinking under his anger. Normally she challenges Nic, so I'm left guessing what changed. I'm concerned to say the least. But no one is ever here except us, so he can get over his shit. I'll fuck my girl where I please.

"Both of you get cleaned up, Dr. Carter is here and waiting in Chelsey's room," Nic commands like we are one of his staff, but with Dr. Carter waiting, now is not the time to argue.

"Fine, Whatever Nic," I grumble as he walks back out the door.

Turning back to Chelsey, she looks almost fearful, and my gut churns at the sight.

Reaching down, I hand her my shirt before tipping her chin up and kissing her lightly.

"All is well Little Bird. Nic is just being a grumpy ass. You ready to meet Dr. Carter?"

"No, but I know I have to be. I can handle Nic being mad at me." She pauses, letting out a deep breath. "But to think I got you in trouble with him because I came in here... I guess I just feel guilty I caused an issue."

A warm smile forms on my face. This woman is not only a warrior but also a bleeding heart for those she cares about, and somehow I made the list.

"Nic is just stressed from work and is being a jerk to everyone. You haven't caused any issues. Now let's go meet Dr. Carter," I say winking at her before leading her out the gym door.

Chapter 12
Chelsey

"Hello Chelsey, I'm Dr. Carter." She extends her hand out for me to shake it.

Dr. Carter is younger than I was expecting. She appears to only be in her mid forties and is tall with brown pixie cut hair. Her thin pencil heels with a tight business formal blue dress on scream professional, while her stethoscope around her neck screams doctor. Her medical bag is already sitting on the bed next to where I sit.

Taking her hand, I shake it politely. "It's nice to meet you." I offer her a kind smile.

"Now Mr. Romano told me you are wanting to get your next birth control shot and have a burn for me to look at, is that correct?" She begins digging in her bag, but stops when I don't answer right away.

"Yes, that's right." I quickly say meeting Nico's gaze.

He is leaning against the wall, watching and listening in silence. He came in here with me, when the other guys stayed in the hall. I didn't want to cause a scene, but I feel nervous with him staring at me. Will he at least turn around when she puts the needle in my ass?

The doctor clears her throat, then follows my gaze to where Nico is standing.

"Mr. Romano, I think Chelsey is nervous to have you in here. Could you please give us a few minutes?" Her voice is gentle as she gestures to the door.

"No. I will be staying." He gives her a stern and tight stare.

Shit. Why couldn't I have just pretended he wasn't here? Now there is going to be this big issue and all because I got nervous. I don't know him well, but I know his type and you don't challenge that type of man.

"No! He can stay." I half shouted desperately.

They both whirl to look at me. Surprise lights Nico's face, his eyebrows slightly raised, but the good doctor still has her eyebrows knitted together and her mouth is pressed into a flat line.

"Chelsey, I have been the Romano family's doctor for years. I can kick Nic out. He will be mad of course, but I will not lose anything by doing so." She steps towards me, grabbing both of my hands, staring down into my eyes. "You are my patient today and you need to speak freely with me. That being said, would you like him to leave the room?"

I look over her shoulder to Nico still leaning on the wall. He is tense. Every muscle is tight, his arms are folded across his chest, and he may be leaning on the wall, but he still has a bodyguard type stance.

He's an ass and I should kick him out just to spite him, but there is something in his eyes. Something he is hiding behind a thick wall, yet still visible in his eyes. He's concerned. He is not here to be controlling, but because he cares, I'd bet my life on it.

The realization shakes me to my core, because it is far easier to believe he is nothing but a controlling dick-head like the majority of the men in this world. But now, I can see the truth, that behind the thick exterior he actually does care.

"Thank you Dr. Carter, but I would like him to stay."

She nods and goes back to her bag.

"Now, let's start by having a look at your burn." I hold out my arm and she examines it carefully. "It doesn't look serious. Keep it clean and use a burn cream."

"Okay. I can do that." I nod and swallow hard as anxiety starts to fill me about what comes next.

"Next order of business, you're wanting your next birth control shot, correct?"

My muscles tighten and I shift uncomfortably.

"Yes, that is the easiest form of birth control for me."

She looks down at me with an assessing stare.

"You seem a bit nervous still, if you have had this before why are you nervous?" Concern laces her voice.

My eyes turn and lock with Nico's and he nods slightly towards me. I'm not sure if that was his way of telling me it's okay to show fear, or if he was giving me permission. But oddly enough it gave me some comfort.

"I'm afraid of needles," I mutter the confession.

In this world fear is a tool to be used against you, I've known this since I was a child. I may have been answering the doctor's question, but I was telling Nico. Confessing it to him.

Nico's firm face softens and his muscles relax a little. My confession must have been a peace offering in some way.

"Oh okay, well have you thought about other options?"

"Yes, this is truly the best option for me." I sigh a little, but there is resolve in my voice.

"Okay, well before I can administer it I need a quick urine sample." She hands me a cup and I head to the bathroom.

Moments later, I arrive back, hand her the cup, and she runs a quick pregnancy test on it. It's routine, but I'm always slightly nervous it will come out positive. Thankfully, it is negative once again.

"While I draw this up, please lay on the bed on your side, with your pants lowered to about halfway down your hips."

Nervous tingles hit my stomach and I feel ready to vomit. Moving to my side, I purposely choose to face away from her. If I see the needle, I may actually vomit.

Breathe, one two three. Just breathe. I repeat my mantra, pinching my eyes closed. I have had this done every three months for years, but every time I am just as scared as the first time.

"Okay, are you ready Chelsey?" Dr. Carter's voice soothes.

"Yes." My voice comes out shaky. *As ready as I'll ever be.*

A cold alcohol swab rubs my hip and I suck in a nervous breath, pinching my eyes closed as tight as they will go.

A warm soft hand suddenly encompasses mine, and my eyes fly open. Nico is not only holding my hand, but is mere inches from my face.

His gaze is steady and full of comfort. "I'm here, I've got you Mio Tesoro." Nico's words are musical and peaceful.

I grip his hand and nod. I have no clue what he just called me, but I know he has me right now and I can trust in that.

He nods to the doctor and the prick of the needle and burn of the medication cause me to suck in a breath, but my eyes never leave Nico's.

"Okay all done." Dr. Carter wipes my cheek with gauze. "Do you need anything else before I leave?"

I shift and Nico helps me sit up. "No I'm all set. Thank you Dr. Carter." I turn to smile at her and she smiles back.

"Okay. You have a great rest of your day and I'm sure I will see you all again soon." And with that, she walks out of the room leaving Nico and I alone.

Chapter 13

Nico

S eeing her scared and vulnerable broke something in me. I know she's just here to stay out of her father's hands, but that fear I just saw was real, and I couldn't let her suffer that alone. Not when she is my responsibility.

She views me as this controlling ass, but in this room right now, she is seeing deeper than just my exterior. She knows that I care for her even though I shouldn't. She knows I'm more than what she has seen from me. Her gaze somehow pierced my soul...

I don't believe in soul mates or fate, but I can't deny this current that draws me too her.

Clearing my throat, I rub her hand. "Are you okay?" My voice is smooth, and that is a rarity for me. I don't do soft things, but something about her softens even my roughest edges.

"Yes, thank you for being with me." Her eyes continue to search mine. And I'm both terrified and drawn to the vulnerability of all of this.

"Okay then. I'll leave you to it." I begin to turn away, but she squeezes my hand. I didn't realize we were still holding hands...

"Nic wait. Please." She stands in front of me and looks up at me. "I know we haven't been on good terms really since I arrived. Especially since I tried to leave, and I just want to say I'm sorry for smacking you when I had my first nightmare here." She wets her lips slightly, dropping her gaze from mine. She is showing her venerability to me, like I have to her. My brows furrow, because I've given her no reason to even want to apologize to me for that. "I don't think you were being a controlling dick, but rather you were scared for me."

I squeeze her hand slightly as something in my chest tightens.

How can she see straight through me, see what I've hidden so carefully... My heart.

Without thought, my emotions cloud my judgment and I kiss her hard, sparks alighting across my skin. I've denied myself any part of her for so long, but no more. I want to claim every part of her as mine.

Forcing her lips apart, my tongue invades her mouth and fuck does she taste better than the finest bourbon.

She moans, pressing her body into me. Her fingers lace into my hair, deepening this maddening kiss.

Pulling back from her, I rest my forehead on hers., "You don't want this with me. I won't play nice with you like my brothers Chelsey. I want to fuck you so hard you feel me for days. I want to fucking destroy you." My voice is deep and husky with need for her.

I expect her to pull away. My words are not sweet, but rude and crass just like I am. This girl likes being doted on and cherished; I'm not her taste.

She drops to her knees and is undoing my belt faster than I can stop her. Do I really want to stop her though? I mean the obvious answer is yes for her sake, but I'm a selfish bastard and I've dreamt about fucking that beautiful mouth of hers for weeks.

"Nic, I don't want gentle or playful with you. I want you to fucking annihilate me. Fuck me until I forget my own name."

My cock aches with how hard I am. It's been so long since I have gotten laid, but this feels like more than a casual fuck and it's a little unnerving.

She pulls me free and stares up at me, mouth parted slightly, a hungry fire in her eyes.

I grip her silk soft hair, pulling back so her head is tilted up fully to me. "You're going to take every inch of my cock in that naughty little mouth aren't you."

Her pupils are blown, and she wets her lips before letting out a shaky breath. "Yes, sir."

My cock jumps at her words. "Then be a good girl and get to work."

I loosen my hold slightly as she takes me into her mouth. I groan loudly as she takes every inch of me, as I hit the back of her throat. I tighten my grip on her hair once more as her fingers claw at my hips as I relentlessly fuck her beautiful mouth.

"Shit *Mio Tesoro*. You look so fucking good taking my cock."

She moans around me, as I swipe a stay tear from her eyes. I want to spill down her slender throat so fucking bad, but I won't. I've wanted to fuck this woman since I met her and I'm not missing my opportunity to fill her pussy.

Releasing her head and pulling myself from her mouth, she gasps, staring up at me with red cheeks and watery eyes. *God, what a gorgeous fucking sight.*

Yanking her to stand upright, I remove her shirt first, then her shorts, and fuck did God make a masterpiece with her body. It's better than I remember. Her large breasts, curvy hips, and thick thighs that I just want to take a bite out of.

Chelsey seems to know what she wants as she claws at my shirt, half ripping it off my body, and I'm more than happy to grant her wish of fucking her until she forgets her name.

Shoving her onto the bed, I grab her legs and drag her to the edge. I have yet to touch that beautiful pussy of hers, and she is already drenched for me. I can see her juices glistening off of her thighs from here.

"Chelsey, you're already fucking soaked." I groan as I lower my face mere inches from her slick folds, smelling her delicious scent. "Are you a dirty little slut for my cock already?"

"Nic, don't tease me... fuck me!" she moans and begs at the same time. Her body arching and turning. She's so damn desperate for my touch.

Wish granted. I began feasting on her and my God, my brother was not lying about how sweet she tastes. This very well could be my favorite meal. Sweet as a fucking summer peach.

She tries to arch up, but I won't allow her to move. I press her down as I suck and flick her swollen clit, then run my tongue to her entrance and slide it in, only to return to her sweet bundle of nerves.

She laces her fingers in my hair as I build her to the precipice of her orgasm.

"Oh God, Nic, don't stop." She mewls.

But I don't take orders from her.

Without giving her any warning, I grab her waist and flip her onto her belly, pulling her round ass up towards me.

My cock aches with how hard I am.

"Nic..."

My name sounds so fucking good being whined out of her.

Slowly, I insert two fingers into her tight entrance and begin pumping in and out. She starts thrusting on them, fucking herself as she chases the high building in her.

I want to feel her come around my fingers, but she has been far too much of a brat for me to reward her with that.

I lean down and sink my teeth into her beautiful ass, and she squeals with both pain and pleasure. Her thighs start to quiver and I know she is close. I remove my fingers, then lick them clean, savoring her taste.

"Nic... No Please! Nic I'm right there!" She bellows.

"You have been nothing but a brat to me since you got here. I only let good girls come."

She whimpers and moans, before I slam my dick into her tight cunt in one thrust. She screams out and I take hold of her throat, holding her head up.

"I told you, I'm not gentle." My voice is so gravelly with the intensity of this.

"Hard Nic. Please fuck me hard." Her voice is desperate as I hold her steady, not allowing her to bounce off my cock like she is trying to.

I'm not sure what kind of response I was expecting, but that was not it. I just denied her a climax and then slammed into her, and now she is begging for more? Fuck if this girl isn't the death of me, she might just be made for me.

"Careful what you ask for." I pull out almost to the tip and slam into her hard.

With every thrust she screams and it's the perfect twisted melody to my ears. She is getting close as the tingles in my lower spine start.

"Promise to be a good girl for me and I'll let you come."

"Yes... Please... I'll be a good girl," She mewls.

"Yeah you will be my good girl."

Her walls quiver and grip my cock like a vise as her climax crashes through her.

"Fuck. Nic!" she bellows in a pleasureful cry

Two more thrusts and I spill into her joining her in the post-fucked oblivion.

"Shit... Chelsey!"

I release her and she collapse on the bed, and I join her. Allowing my brain to come down from it all. That may have been the best lay of my life. I've fucked a lot of woman, but none have ever taken anything and everything I throw at them and then begged for more.

Sitting up, I slide on my boxers and grab my clothes before heading for the door. I know it's a dick move not to stay with her, but that was intense and to stay with her after would only make all my feelings too much. I need to get away and clear my head.

She stares at me on the bed. "Thanks for the comfort and making me forget my name." Her voice is musical, and she smiles at me. I was just as mean to her in that bed as I've been since she got here and now she is smiling at me. Fuck, maybe this woman is perfect.

Chapter 14
Chelsey

"It's my turn to cook this morning!" I admonish Enzo, bumping him with my hip.

"I know, but I figured I could just do it. You were sleeping so peacefully." He smiles down at me, making my chest fill with warmth.

"Well, thank you." I reach up and peck his cheek, before moving to the coffee pot. I take a mug from the cupboard and begin filling it, as Nic strides into the kitchen in his gray sweatpants, and missing a shirt.

A week has gone by since we fucked each other's brains out and he hasn't made a move to take me again, but things are different between us, you could almost call it civil even.

"Coffee?" I ask, lifting the pot.

"Sure, thanks," he grumbles as he takes a seat at the corner table.

Whatever Nic and I shared was glorious, and the intensity caused me to have the best orgasm of my life. I knew he would be rough in bed, but I didn't realize I would love it as much as I did. I was sore for days just like he promised.

He cared when I was afraid and I trusted him in that, but what we shared was not caring. It was rough, filled with need and pure lust.

He may show moments of his tender heart, but I can't let my guard down. It's weird but I have fond feelings for Marco and Enzo, and I know those feelings are safe with them.

With Nic, those feelings would be anything but safe, not that it will stop me from seeking pleasure from him.

I pour him a cup of coffee and walk it over to him, setting it down, and leaning forward enough to give him a peak below my shirt. He leans back in his seat with a tilted smirk on his face.

"I know what you're doing."

"I'm not doing anything." I bat my eyes and stand straighter.

"If your craving a little punishment, all you need to do is ask Chelsey." He takes a sip of his coffee and raises an eyebrow at me.

"Like I said, I'm not doing anything." I smile then turn, walking away with an extra swish to my hips.

He lets out a loud sigh, telling me exactly what I wanted to know. I'm getting under that skin of his.

Walking back to Enzo, I wrap my arms around his waist, and he tucks me into his side in response. "As much as I love the idea of having you as my sous chef, you should go get Marco. Breakfast is almost done."

I reach up and kiss him and his hand cups my backside holding me to him.

"Go get Marco, Chelsey!" Nic barks from the corner. "I don't want burnt eggs this morning."

Doing as I'm told, I move away from Enzo and meet Nico's gaze. "Yes, sir," I say as meekly as possible and his eyes blow wide.

Bating my eyes one last time, I leave to get Marco, who I assume is in his room since I haven't seen him yet this morning.

I get to his door and knock lightly, before sliding inside. He is asleep on his bed, flat on his back with an arm thrown off the side.

Quietly I tiptoe to the empty side of the bed and climb in beside him. He groans at the intrusion and his eyes peal open, meeting mine. A tired smile crosses his lips and he pulls me to him immediately.

"Zo has breakfast almost done."

"Breakfast can wait, I want to enjoy snuggling you," he grumbles and I run my finger through his hair and over his neck.

"It can't though. I'm pretty sure Zo or Nic will come in here looking for us if we don't go out soon."

He groans, and kisses me. Fireworks explode over my skin and I never want it to end. Pulling away, he looks at me with a hungry gaze.

"If we don't leave this bed, Little Bird, you will be my breakfast."

"NO FUCKING! GET OUT HERE!" Nic's voice yells down the hall and I snicker into Marco's chest.

"I guess we have our answer to that idea." "Yeah... fucking cock blocking ass-hat." Marco sighs frustrated and climbs from bed.

Each of his muscles flex along his back as he slides on his pants and bite my lower lip. I like Marco's idea for breakfast a little better than the eggs Enzo had going.

Marco turns, catching me ogling him and his eyes narrow.

"Come on." He reaches his hand out to me. "Or your deviant ways are going to land us both in the doghouse."

I climb from the bed, and take his hand. He leads us out of the room and back to the kitchen where Enzo is pulling out plates and Nic is refilling his coffee.

It's all so domestic feeling. Like this is the way life is supposed to be. A contentment washes over me and I move to start making my plate. Marco follows close behind and we all gather at the table, eating our breakfast like a weird almost family.

After breakfast, I head to shower and clean up for the day. I'm starting to realize more and more with each passing day, that the idea of this being temporary is getting harder to swallow.

Eventually this will come to an end, and I'm starting to question what will be left of me when it does. I've given a piece of myself to Enzo and Marco. What if I can't take those back?

I allow the water to wash away the fears of the unknown. They say let tomorrow worry about itself and that is what I'm choosing to do. *I'll enjoy this for as long as I can.*

Done, I go to my dresser and find a cute pair of panties with peaches on it. Chuckling to myself as I slide them on.

A soft knock sounds on the door and Marco strides in. His eyes rake over me and I don't blame him, since I am still only wearing peach panties.

Clearing his throat his eyes shoot to mine. "Enzo will be so disappointed he wasn't here to see you dressing for him." Marco's voice is deep and husky.

"Well, I do aim to please." I wink giving him a seductive smile.

Seriously, who am I becoming? I'm like a sex crazed teenage boy when it comes to these men.

Marco's eyes darken and I can see the bulge in his pants, but he doesn't move. "You have no idea how bad I want to rip those little panties off of you right now"

"Then why don't you?" I toss my hair over my shoulder to fully expose myself to him.

He closes the space between us and his hands come up, kneading my breasts. My sex already throbbing with need.

Slowly, he slides one hand down my body, dipping into my panties. "Your already dripping for me."

"Yes..."

He inserts a finger into my center, and I moan pressing myself into him.

"Already so needy for my cock." He growls, covering my lips with his, but pulls back, leaving me desperate for more. "I'm sorry, not right now. I need you to get dressed."

I whine in frustration as he steps back from me.

Get dressed? I don't think I have been fully dressed in something other than t-shirts and panties or cotton shorts since my first time with Marco. Confusion must be etched on my face, because he is smiling at me.

"We have the night off, since the club is getting some repairs done this evening. So we are taking our girl out on a proper date."

A smile plasters across my face, and I run to him, wrapping my arms around his neck.

"Really?" I squeal with excitement. "Don't get me wrong I love hanging out here with all of you, but a real date sounds incredible!" I release him and bounce over to the fully stocked closet, Marco chuckling behind me.

He can laugh all he wants, but I have never been on an actual date, or at least one I cared about.

"Where are we going? How should I dress?" I turn to face him, bouncing on my heels.

"Chelsey, I cannot take you seriously when you make your tits bounce like that."

"Maarrcoooo," I drone impatiently for my answer.

"Okay, I'm under strict instructions not to give anything away." He holds his hands up in surrender. "All I'll tell you is to wear something casual and comfortable, but fit for a public outing."

"Like a casual summer dress or jeans with sneakers?"

"Nope, that is all you'll be getting out of me Little Bird. Get ready and meet us in the kitchen." He turns on his heels and walks out of my room.

A little while later I stare at myself in my mirror, praying I'm dressed appropriately. The baby pink dress is covered with white daisies and it flows around me beautifully. My hair is tied back in a simple braid and only light make-up dot's my cheeks, giving myself a beautiful glow.

My boys are taking me out on a real date and while excitement bounces through me, I'm also a bit nervous. I want this to be fun and dreamy but I'd be kidding myself if I thought for a moment that Nico or Marco could be romantic.

Sliding on my flat sandals, I leave my room.

Passing through the living room, I hear Marco and Enzo talking in the kitchen and warmth blooms in my chest. I want to feel Enzo's hands around me, and Marco's lips on mine. I'm yanked from my thoughts when a hand wraps around my throat, and I'm pulled back to a hard wall of muscle.

"I'm here to take you on a date, but this dress is just going to get you fucked *Mio Tesoro.*" Nico's deep, hungry voice vibrates through me and I want to fucking melt for him, but not now, we have a date.

"Maybe I want to be fucked."

He growls in my ear, pressing his already hard length to my backside, causing heat to pool in my core. These men always make me so needy for them and I'm playing a dangerous game by teasing him.

Marco and Enzo file in from the kitchen and my insides scream at the idea that this may turn to an all out fuck fest!

"Nic, if I'm banned from touching her then so are you!" Marco jeers.

"Yeah, plus I already have everything packed. Stop touching her and lets go." Enzo joins in and I have to keep myself from pouting when I realize this isn't going back to the bedroom.

Nico reluctantly releases me, and Enzo quickly drags me away.

We make our way to the kitchen where a picnic basket sits on the counter and a new sense of excitement washes over me.

"A picnic?"

"Yes. Just something simple and intimate for us to enjoy each other," Marco says next to my ear as he wraps his arms around me from behind.

"What are we waiting for? Let's go!" I pull from his arms and bounce to the elevator as Nic chuckles besides me.

He actually chuckled. And it causes a soft, sense of pride to fill me, knowing I brought it out in him.

The elevator feels like it's moving at a turtle's speed to the garage, and the boys- My boys are sporting proud smiles, even Nic has a soft one.

Finally reaching the garage, they lead me to the SUV I was first picked up in and Nic climbs in the front to drive while Enzo, Marco, and I sandwich ourselves in the back. Of course I'm in the middle, right where I want to be.

I lean into Marco's side, as Enzo rubs dotting circles over my hand with his thumb. This could be so much hotter, but I'm to focused on where we are going to pay much mind to the fact they are both so close.

Nic drives us through the city and pulls the car to a stop on the side of the road in front of a beautiful park.

"You ready?" he asks, turning to see me smiling from ear to ear.

"Yes."

"Alright, let's go then."

Enzo and Marco climb out the side doors and I follow Enzo out the left side, where Nic is waiting for me.

He takes my hand and laces his fingers with mine, leading me to the back of the car where Marco is grabbing the large wicker picnic basket from the trunk and Enzo is holding a large red blanket.

I follow the three of them as they lead us to the not yet chosen spot. The sun warms my skin as it shines through the large oak trees. The squirrels are scampering about and the birds are whistling. I couldn't think of a more beautiful spot or a nicer day for a picnic.

Enzo stops in a large meadow like clearing with flowers scattered about and throws out the blanket.

He walks over to me with something deep in his eyes I can't quite read. "What do you think of this spot sweet girl?"

"I think it's perfect."

"Thank fuck!" Marco says dropping the basket on to the blanket. "I thought that asshole was going to make us walk another mile."

"Quit whining like a little baby," Nico orders but not in a serious way. There is a lightness to him, to all of us really.

"You try carrying a basket packed to the brim with food for four people, then tell me how your arms feel, Nic," Marco jeers as he flexes and stretches his biceps.

Walking over, I take a seat in front of him on the blanket. "Not too sore to hold me I hope." I look at him and flutter my eyes in a way I know he won't be able to resist. Within a second he plops down behind me and pulls me to his lap.

"I could be on my deathbed, and I'd still use the last of my strength to hold you." He kisses the top of my head and Nic rolls his eyes sitting across from us.

"Such a sap," Nic teases but I have this feeling deep within that even though Marco said it, they all mean it too.

Enzo pulls things from the basket. A clear swing top water bottle with cups, plates, a bowl with grapes and strawberries, and what appear to be BLT sandwiches. My mouth waters at the display in front of us. This could not be a more perfect day.

Grabbing a strawberry from the bowl, I put it in my mouth, taking a bite and pursing my lips around it. All of their eyes bore into me, butterflies and heat blooming in my core. I love the power I wield with these men.

Nic picks up a strawberry and holds it in front of me. "Eat another." His voice now low and husky.

I do as I'm told but lick my lips when I'm finished, letting out a soft moan.

Nic holds my gaze, and I lean forward slightly. His mouth tips up and my breathing picks up as heat floods every inch of me. Who knew a picnic could be so sensual. I don't know if I'm nervous, in love, or desperate to be fucked!

Enzo breaks the growing tension clearing his throat and passing out the sandwiches, and I force myself to break my eyes away from Nico's.

"This looks so good. Thank you Zo." I smile before taking a bite of my food.

"I'm happy to serve Sweet Peach." He winks at me and takes a bite of his food. Marco and Nic quickly doing the same.

My heart couldn't be more content. This whole thing feels like a blissful dream, and I just bask in their presence as we enjoy our meal.

Before me is the best trifecta. Nico. The strong alpha male, with a large heart lying beneath the surface. Enzo. The soft gooey bleeding heart, but strong and protective. Marco. The playful one, but fiercely loyal. They are all so different, yet together they make a beautiful and dangerous force, and somehow for some reason they have brought me into the mix.

"My turn," Enzo teases yanking me to my feet as soon as I finish the last of my food. "Come on, I want to show you something."

Marco rolls his eyes as Nic grumbles something inaudible under his breath. I look to him with furrowed brows hoping he will share, but he only nods towards Enzo.

I bring my attention back to Enzo and lace my fingers through his as he leads me through the field to a small pond.

It's almost clear enough to see the bottom, small fish swimming though out it as lily pads rest on the surface. Rocks are scatted around the waters edge with cat-tails and other tall grass sticking up towards the back.

"It's beautiful," I whisper in awe of the simple beauty of it.

"It is."

We stand in silence just resting in the peacefulness of this place.

"Sometimes I come here when things feel a bit too heavy to carry. The work we do isn't always safe or legal and I've always found looking at the water helps lighten the load a little."

"I can see why. This place makes the world feel smaller." Releasing his hand, I walk to the waters edge. Then dip my hand in, letting all the coolness of the water wash over my skin. "Thank you for bringing me here Zo."

He smiles at me with one of those smiles that says more than words could ever say. One that speaks of feelings deep below the surface.

"I wanted to share my place with you and we all wanted to show you exactly what you mean to us."

Walking back to him, I lace my fingers with his once more and kiss him softly.

"Can we head back to the others now?"

"Of course, my Sweet Peach."

He tucks a stray hair behind my ear, and we begin our walk over to the guys. When they come into view Nico is hitting Marco in the nose with a strawberry in what appears to be an attempt to make it into his mouth.

"My turn?" I yell, stealing both of their attentions.

Nico stands and walks over to us. "Nope. Enzo had his walk, now you're mine."

My breathing shallows. "What?"

Enzo chuckles and kisses my hand, then drops it. "Have fun, Sweet Peach." He jogs away over to Marco and the rest of our stuff.

"Let's go," Nico's firm voice commands and I roll my eyes as he gestures in a westward direction.

I begin walking and he's at my side, his hands relaxed next to him. We haven't spent much alone time together, and this feels both good and concerning at the same time.

"Where are we going?" I ask trying to watch his face, but he remains facing forward.

"You'll see."

"Nic, please just tell me what's going on." My voice shakes slightly with my anxiety.

"You know this is part of what pisses me off about you." He doesn't pause, just keeps walking and my brows crease with confusion. "You have balls of fucking steel when shit gets dangerous, but any other time your soft and quick to scare." He says it with tenderness, telling me it's not an insult, but I don't know what the fuck it is.

He steps in front of me and our eyes lock. Anticipation and my growing anxiety coil in my stomach as I stare at his firm features.

"Chelsey, you've never been safer and more in danger than you are with me." He drops my gaze only for a second. I can see his walls wavering, threatening to show his vulnerability once more.

"What the hell is that supposed to mean?" My tone is clipped as I try to unweave his words.

"It mean's that you've been under my skin since the moment I met you." It comes out almost like a snarl as he steps towards me, but I don't move back. "But after last week, I can't go a day without craving your taste, or desiring to feel you once more."

His features start to soften, his hand brushing my waist with a light touch. The feeling sends a shiver through me and my anxiety is quickly replaced with a need to touch him.

"It means, that I'll protect you like a member of my household, but also that I want to claim your body as my own. Turn your ass an angry red and fuck you until you can't walk straight." He backs us up until my back hits a tree and his face is mere inches from mine. My body cries with need for him as my center ignites and my sex throbs.

"It means, that if you were smart you would leave me the fuck alone and enjoy my brothers because I feel incapable of leaving you alone any longer."

My heart threatens to beat out of my chest and my breathing shallows. I wet my lips, staring deep into his eyes. He's right, it would be smarter to walk away and just enjoy his brothers, but like him, I feel incapable of leaving him alone. Enzo and Marco should be more than I could ever want and need, but I'm drawn to Nico too.

"Then don't Nic," I whisper and he claims me in a harsh kiss. He forces his tongue into my mouth and I gladly welcome it.

He lifts me and I wrap my legs around his waist as he presses me into the tree, his rock-hard cock grinding into my center. He bites my neck, and I cry out.

"I'm going to take you against this tree, *Mio Tesoro*, and you're going to spend the rest of this date with my cum inside you, knowing full well that you are mine." He growls against my skin and I press myself into him.

"Yours," I whimper.

With one hand he hikes my dress up, then moves to undo his buckle and his cock springs free.

"Wait, we're in a park."

"The whole damn world can watch me claim you, but no one will see what belongs to me," he growls and I nod.

"Claim me, Nic."

He pulls my panties to the side and slams into me.

"Holy shit! More... please," I mewl as he slams into me harder, nailing me to the tree. His thrusts are punishing and I climb higher to my climax.

He grips my breast, pinching my nipple through my bra and I cry out louder.

"Quiet down or you'll get us caught," he commands, and I pinch my mouth shut.

My thighs quake and I rest my head back against the trunk. Nico's hand covers my mouth and my orgasm crashes through me as a hot rush of fluid leaves me.

"Holy fuck, you just squirted all over me... Such a good fucking girl," he rasps as he slams into me and spills so deep inside I feel him in my very center. I mewl into his hand and press back into his cock, taking every last drop he has.

"You're mine now Little *Tesoro*."

"Yours," I say breathless as he lowers me back to my feet and tucks himself away.

Chapter 15
Marco

What is this girl doing to us? She is beyond special and she is changing everything for the better.

I have wined and dined women before, but today with her was one I never wanted to end. We all took our moments with her. Enzo brought her to his "spot," and I got to hold her through dinner. Nic and her went on a walk and came back looking like they worked out their shit, but I didn't miss my Little Bird's post fuck glow and her cum on his pants.

With Chelsey everything just feels right and I'm scared that someday sooner than I would like she won't be with us anymore.

I need to savor this, to savor her.

Back at the apartment, my girl looks like she is on cloud nine. She is nothing but glowing joy and smiles. My chest warms as I pull her to it, breathing in her scent of the breeze and her normal vanilla orange from her shower stuff.

"How about a movie night with all of us? I don't think I'm ready to end date night yet." I say loud enough so my brothers hear too.

"Yeah. We could watch Aquaman two!" Enzo is definitely excited by the idea.

"No." Nic's stern voice ends that idea. "Today has been a lot of fun and I'm not competing against Momoa's muscular tattooed body tonight."

My lips press together trying to contain the laugh in my chest. But Chelsey breaks, laughing hysterically and we all start rolling.

"Nic, are you jealous?" she asks clearly intrigued by this discovery.

"No *Tesoro*. But the only men you are allowed to gawk over are standing in this room."

There is a mischievous glint to her eye. Oh she is going to fuck with him on this, it's just a matter of time.

"Fine, what about Marley and Me?" she offers.

"Aw man. Is that the one where the dog dies?" Enzo throws his hands up in dramatic effect and now I want to laugh at him too.

"Yes, but the story is so good it's worth the ending."

"Fine, but I want no judgment if I cry! It's just wrong to kill the dog."

"I won't judge if you don't." She gives him one of those sweet smiles and I know we're watching that movie.

"Alright, now that you two are finished," Nic laughs. "Enzo get the snacks, Marco set up the movie, Chelsey go get changed into your uniform and meet us on the couch."

"Uniform?" She stares at him with furrowed brows and I'm slightly curious if maybe he has a naughty nurse outfit for her in there or something.

181

"Yea, one of our shirts and a pair of panties. The only thing you ever seem to wear in this place." He tosses her a crooked smile and I release her.

"Yes, sir," she says meekly before walking away with an extra swish to her hips.

Nic sits on the couch while I set the movie up and Enzo comes in with enough snacks to feed an army.

Chips with salsa, popcorn, pretzels, a jar of peanut butter, and my damn cookies... Again.

"No. Go put them back right now." I throw my hand out pointing straight to the kitchen.

"Nope, Chels is going to want them."

"Enzo, those are the one thing sacred in this house for me. She won't miss what she doesn't know about."

"Oh she knows about them."

"I swear to the Lord above-"

Chelsey comes jogging into the room. Tits free beneath my white shirt and black lace panties beneath.

"Oh are those Oreos and peanut butter?" She drops to the couch instantly grabbing them and, well let's just say the idea of my cookies being a scared thing is now total fucked.

Enzo stares at me, "I told you so" written all over his face, but there is a better time to fight with my brother than right now. Tonight I want to enjoy my girl and watch this total chick flick.

After a minute we are all piled on the couch. Chelsey is the middle, leaning against Nic with her legs thrown over Enzo and her feet on my lap. I hit play and allow my mind to wonder if this could be it for us. A life of park dates, movies, fucking, and a damn happy ever after. Damn it, Enzo's sappy shit is starting to rub off on me.

Chapter 16
Chelsey

I'm in bed, reading a sweet romance when a knock sounds on my door, and I sit up. It's late, but maybe one of my little brothers had a nightmare or something.

"Come in," I yell, setting the book on my nightstand.

My father walks in with Tony, and instantly I sit up straighter. I made all my runs successfully this week, turned in my cash, made no trouble. Why are they here. It's never good when my father brings his second.

"Is something wrong?" I ask cooly.

"No dear." My father comes over and brushes a hand over my head. "We are here to talk to you about your new job in the business, now that you're eighteen."

My birthday was three days ago, and it went by without so much as a 'happy birthday' from anyone. I'm surprised he noticed.

"New job?" I ask wearily.

"Yes, you're an adult now and it's time you start fulfilling your role as a woman."

My gut sinks and I'm ready to throw up at what he is insinuating.

"What does that mean?" I need him to say the words...

"You will service my men. Give them a good fuck when they need it."

I clutch my blanket, stuffing down all the anxiety welling in me.

"Tony will start with you tonight. Everyone else is out of the house, so it's the best time to break you in." He shrugs like this is no big deal as tears well in my eyes.

Tony approaches and sits next to me and my eyes widen toward my father. He can't be serious.

"Dad, please. You're not serious."

"Sweetheart. This is what you were made for." He nods then leaves the room.

I turn to Tony, taking off his shirt.

"No. You can't do this to me."

"I have my orders. If you fight, it will only hurt worse."

He stands and takes the blanket from me.

I scream and try to kick him, but he catches my leg.

"Wake up. You're safe, *Mio Tesoro.*"

I'm ripped from the nightmare, wrapped in Nico's arms in my room. Tears well in my eyes, spilling over as I cling to Nic like a lifeline.

"Shhh" he soothes, but the memory is thick.

I curl into him, breathing in his whiskey honey scent, centering myself in the feel of his strong arms. The tears stop but Nico holds me close.

"What was your dream, *Tesoro*?"

I take a shaky breath, I've never told anyone before. A lot suspect, but I've never shared my nightmares.

"It was about the first time my father made me fuck one of his men... His second in command raped me. Stole my virginity." It's all I can bear to say.

Nico goes stiff as board but stays quiet. Fear that he will reject me now knowing this about me floods my brain. I wouldn't blame him.

"He will be dealt with." Nic lifts my chin to meet his gaze. It's soft, filled with something deeper than words can describe. "*Mio Tesoro*, it's not our trauma that defines us but how we overcome it. We all have our scars. But you need to keep fighting those demons that never sleep and we will be here to hold you when you feel weak."

I nod and silent tears fall once more as he cradles me to his chest and I drift back to sleep.

· • ● ● ● • ● ● • • ·

I wake up alone, still feeling the after shock of last nights dream. They never get easier, but the guys make the aftereffects better.

Locking away my feelings, I make my way to the kitchen. I'm starving, so I get started on making myself some eggs and toast. I heard the music in the gym, so I'm assuming that is where Marco is. Nic will definitely be in his office, and I'm not sure where Enzo is.

No one finds me during breakfast and I decide that once I finish with dishes, it's time to pester Marco a little.

As I wash the last dish a very hot and sexy version of Nic walks into the kitchen in nothing but black basketball shorts, sweat sprinkling his skin. I'm definitely gawking as he grabs a glass of water from the fridge door.

"If you scrub that plate much more, it'll be more sterile than a hospital operating room."

Fuck. Yeah I was just caught.

"Oh, yeah it had food stuck on it." *Lame excuse Chelsey.*

"Sure it did." He walks over standing dangerously close.

Heat floods my core as an image of him fucking me on this counter flashes through my mind, but he makes no move to touch me. Only taunts me, giving me nothing but a knowing smirk.

"I got work to tend to *Mio Tesoro*. But we all have to go to the club tonight and you're coming too. Dress fitting for a night with us."

He takes another long swig of his water, before walking away. Leaving me wet, needy, and a little shocked by the prospect of going to the club.

· • ● ● ● • ● ● ● • ·

Holy shit! Maybe this dress is too much. I stare at myself in the mirror and I look hot as hell. The black dress covered in sparkles is so short it only goes to my mid thigh. Form fitting with spaghetti straps and a huge V in the middle that damn near goes down to my navel. I'm not sure if the boys will like how much skin this shows and I'm a little worried I may fall out of it.

I did my make-up to compliment it and worked some magic with my hair. I have it pinned off to the side with loose curls. I'm definitely club ready, but am I club ready when being accompanied by three powerful, sexy men?

With flutters in my belly, I venture from my room and find all three Romano brothers dressed in full suits waiting for me in the kitchen, and I can't help but smile at the sight of them.

Zo sees me first and smacks Marco on the shoulder to get his attention. He looks at me like how I would imagine a charming prince looking at a princess. He looks down right awed and sparkles shower from his eyes as he stares at me.

Marco's eyes rake over me as he starts rubbing his jaw. A crooked smirk forms on his face and I know he is thinking about how easy it would be for him to relieve me of this dress.

Heat floods my cheeks under their stares, and my stomach won't stop doing back flips. I've been to clubs before, but I've always dressed a little more modestly. Always trying to avoid my dad and his men's attention, but I definitely wanted these guy's attention. And I most definitely have it.

Turning my attention to Nic, his eyes are dark with desire. He rakes his hand through his hair and heat floods my core. *I want to do that.*

Nic is the first to move and when he approaches he slowly circles me, hands in his pockets as he inspects me. "You look absolutely ravenous in that dress. But take care tonight. If you fall out of that napkin you're wearing I'll give you the spanking of your life." My breath hitches at his words as heat sears between my thighs. *I kind of want that spanking...* "Do you understand me?"

"Yes sir," I coo and his eyes flare at my words. I love that I already have power over this man and he certainly doesn't want me knowing that.

"Okay you two. We have work to get to," Marco teases as he pulls Nic towards the elevator.

Enzo wraps an arm around my waist, whispering in my ear, "Be careful Sweet Peach. Don't push Nic too far or you'll end up bent over his desk." Then leads me to the elevator.

How am I going to make it through tonight? I feel hot as hell, these men are all drop dead gorgeous, and I'm so damn needy after the promises — threats — made this evening. I mean come on, how could I not look forward to the potential of being fucked over the club desk or the maddening spanking that will guarantee the best orgasms.

We pile into the black car just outside the building, and I'm sandwiched between Marco and Enzo. Nico sits across from me relaxed with his legs spread a little, but his eyes are still dark and pinned on me.

"At the club, we will be helping with security. Marco you will be at the bar area, Enzo the left side of the dance floor, and I will be on the upper floor." The boys nod their agreements and Nic leans forward on his knees. "Chelsey, you're to be with one of us at all times. Do you understand?" His voice is commanding with steel in his gaze, but I'm in no mood for his ass-hat attitude.

Repressing my smile, I lean forward on my knees getting mere inches from his face. I'm not sure what is prompting the sudden boldness I feel. Maybe it's the sexy as fuck dress. Maybe it's the fact that I thoroughly enjoy being naked with these men. But the idea of getting under Nic's skin right now is damn near intoxicating.

"Yes, I understand." I keep my voice meek and bat my eyes at him.

Nic eyes me with his own skepticism, like he knows the game I'm trying to play. The question is, will he play too? *God, I hope so.*

Moments later we stop in front of a large club with people lining the street three blocks down to get in. I know who these men are, but I'm a little shocked by the scale of this club. It has to be one of the biggest in Seattle.

"Let's go," Nico barks and we climb out of the car. Marco offers me his hand to help me out, but the people have my attention. We are not overdressed by any standards. Some women are actually revealing more skin than I am, which is impressive since this dress doesn't cover much.

I shift on my feet waiting for Nic and Enzo to exit the car. These women are gorgeous and their bodies are perfect. *Everything I'll never be.* They are all skinny with perfect hair, and make-up done to look like every guy's dream. They're all probably super flexible yoga instructors or some shit to boot.

"I could get plenty of women at the club we own" Marco's words fill my head. I won't ever measure up to these women.

My face falls and I look to the ground as reality cements into my brain and it hurts. These are the women they like and my curvy body is just a play break for a minute. *This won't last...* Damn it, when did I start wanting it to?

Marco grabs my chin and lifts it up to meet his eyes. "Little Bird, if you're that disappointed we didn't strip you naked in the car there is always the ride home."

Stuff down the hurt Chels. You have this time with them now.

"Is that a promise?" I tease back ignoring the ache in my chest.

A devilish grin spreads across his face as Enzo presses against my back.

"Oh that solely depends on your behavior this evening. Push Nic too far Sweet Peach and you might not make it to the car before your clothes leave," Enzo whispers in my ear and my breath hitches. That's right, I have a game to play.

Chapter 17
Enzo

E veryone knows me as the gentle one, the caretaker if you will, and I've always preferred more intimacy with sex than my brothers do. But I do like to play games and as soon as my Sweet Peach walked into the kitchen this evening I knew she wanted to play.

Right now her goal is to get under Nic's skin, she's a far cry from hiding those intentions, and fuck does Nic look ready to play as well.

My plan is simple. I want them both worked up. I want Nic ready to claim every inch of her and join us for the fun this evening. With Chelsey, I want her so fucking hot for us that she becomes down right desperate. Anticipation fills me, it's sure to be a hell of a good game.

We make our way to the entrance, and Mark is ever the gentleman and opens the door for us. "Good evening sirs." His voice is monotone and flat, his eyes never leaving the crowd. We don't respond. At the club we are all business.

As always, the place is filled to capacity, our DJ playing some upbeat techno stuff. Chelsey looks so incredibly vibrant under the neon lights and I know my brothers have noticed as well. How could they not, she is a damn goddess this evening.

"Alright, get your ear pieces in and get to your posts now," Nico barks us and I just roll my eyes. He's always been a gruff asshole, but right now he's extra assholey thanks to Chelsey.

"Aye Aye Captain," Chelsey mocks and I whirl to stare at her. She is wearing a teasing smile, moving her hand to her forehead to salute him and I bust out laughing, unable to contain myself. This girl is truly something else and my chest swells with pride that she actually just did that.

Nic pins her daggers and gets so close their chests are touching, and she just stares up at his growling face. "Pick someone to go with now."

"I told you I understood in the car."

Nic's so tense, he looks downright ready to snap already. But it's far too early for this game to end.

"Alright Sweet Peach, you're with me for now. To the dance floor you go." I smile at Nic and pull her close

"See you soon Nic," she tosses over her shoulder, batting her eyes at him. Oh she's most definitely going to be getting spanked this evening, and I'm pretty sure that's her goal.

Out on the dancefloor, people are staring. Women gawk at me, which is not unusual, but men are staring tonight too. And they're staring at my woman, and I don't like it one bit.

I'm not the possessive claiming type, but she's still mine and if she lets anyone of these dickheads here touch her, she will see the side of me I keep under lock and key. And whoever touched her would probably lose their hand or more from one of my brothers.

"You see that Sweet Peach?" I turn her to face the men staring at her. "You let any of those men touch you and you won't like the consequences," I whisper the warning in her ear.

She turns away from the guys and faces me. "Zo... are you jealous right now?" She eyes me playfully, but in this matter I'm far from fucking playing

I yank her towards me, so my chest is touching hers and tip her chin, so her eyes meet mine. "I can't be jealous over what's already mine, and no one touches what belongs to the Romanos." Her breathing hitches as she presses into me harder.

"Yes, no one touches what belongs to the Romanos. No one will touch me, Zo." She utters her words softly almost like a promise, but it's the exact choice of words she chose that have my brain doing back flips.

"Alright. Now go shake that ass on the dance floor for me."

Her eyes twinkle with excitement and she jumps up, kisses me quickly, then bounces off to the dance floor with a beaming smile, that damn near brings me to my knees.

I'm supposed to be here for security tonight and I guess I am in a way. I'm Chelsey Ryan's personal bodyguard, because I cannot take my eyes off of her. She is dancing like no one is watching; I have never seen her so carefree.

The next song is hot and heavy. The couples on the floor are practically having sex and Chelsey is eyeing me like she wants me to join her. She points at me and wiggles her finger for me to go to her. Well, I'm here with a mission tonight and this may be the best possible opportunity and it fell right into my lap.

I walk out onto the floor, and people part like the Red Sea. When I get to my Sweet Peach she doesn't say a word, just spins around and glues her perfect round ass to my already half hard cock, and starts grinding on me.

"Fuck Chelsey, your so damn intoxicating," I groan into the side of her neck as my hands travel along all the skin this dress of hers doesn't cover. She half giggles and half moans. She knows exactly what the hell she's doing, and she has me ready to fuck her right here on the dance floor.

Later... I will fuck her into oblivion later. I purposefully drag my eyes away from my girl, scanning for my brothers. For the love of all that is good, please let them be watching.

I spot Marco first and he is scowling with jealousy as he stares at us. When my eyes lock with his, he shakes his head like he knows what I'm up to.

"Enzo. My office now! Bring that fucking brat with you," Nico's gruff stern voice fills my earpiece and I smile ear to ear.

Mission accomplished. Nico is so wound up he is about to snap and wherever he is, he's definitely watching.

"Chelsey, Nic is requesting an audience in his office. We need to go."

She spins around so fast, drops to the floor, then stands back up slowly running her hands over me all the way up and stopping at my cock that is so damn hard it's practically weeping.

"Nic can wait," she coos, turning back around to grind on me. Fuck me... Getting on Nic's shit list was not part of the plan, but with how she is dancing, it's worth being a target for his wrath.

"Enzo now!" Nico booms over my earpiece.

"Sorry bro, she's refusing to come. You may have to come get us," I tease into my mic.

"Marco get those fuckers and get to my office."

"Of course." Marco sounds way too gratified by the assignment.

"Chelsey darling, our party is about to be interrupted. I think you're about to get that punishment you seem to have been working so hard for."

"I have no clue what you're talking about, Zo." She bites her lower lip and I cannot wait to bite it myself.

Chapter 18
Chelsey

Anticipation fills me as Marco drags me through the club and down a hallway to an office with a door similar to the sound proof one at Players.

"You did it now, Little Bird. Are you ready for what's waiting for you behind that door?" Marco eyes me, searching for any indecisiveness.

Little does he know, this is exactly what I wanted. My stripper skills came in handy on that dance floor tonight.

"Yes." It comes out breathless and I pin my thighs together, heat flooding my core.

He opens the door to Nic leaning over his desk with fire in his eyes. Marco walks me in, and Zo closes the door behind us locking a deadbolt.

"You want to explain whatever the fuck that was on the dancefloor?" Nic's voice booms and pride blossoms in my chest, knowing I worked him up this much.

"Sure. I was dancing like a stripper just for you Sweet Nic." I bat my eyes at him, challenging him to give me his worst.

Nic drops his eyes and runs his tongue over his bottom lip. *Please Nic punish me like you promised.* I shift on my feet, my pussy already needy for what is about to happen.

"Get her naked right fucking now," he growls, untying his tie.

Enzo and Marco are on either side of me in a matter of seconds and they slowly get me out of my dress, then bra, then panties.

"Don't touch her," Nic commands and it about has me ready to beg for forgiveness because I need to be touched right fucking now! My skin is practically searing from the heat I have flowing through me.

Nic walks around his desk shirtless and grabs my face in his large hand. "You want to act like a brat and a little whore, then you will be treated like one."

Yes please!

"First I'm going to spank that ass of yours until it's as red as a damn strawberry. Then my brothers here will get their turn by fucking that cherry red ass and that smart mouth of yours. And then I'm going to take what is mine and fuck you until you only see fucking stars." *Holy shit.* His words have my insides doing back flips and my juices dripping down my thighs.

Nic releases my face. "Now go bend over my desk like a good fucking girl."

He doesn't move as I walk around the back side of his desk. The cool touch of the desktop as I lean over has my body screaming even more. The slow progression of this is the worst torture.

"Marco, Enzo, tie her wrists to the desk legs." Oh. My… The more this goes on the hotter it gets.

Nic kneels in front of me meeting my eyes. Holding his tie. "Pick a safe word *Mio Tesoro*." His sexy as fuck crooked smile plasters his face.

"What?" My eyes widen and my belly flips with a nervous energy. I've never been given a safe word before. I'm not sure if it was the lack of option to make it stop or the lack of needing one, but either way I've never had one.

"Pick. A. Fucking. Safe word."

"PEACHES!" I yell hastily, exacerbated.

"Good choice, Sweet Peach," Enzo coos from my left wrist, wearing a cocky grin.

Without another word. My eyes are covered by Nic's tie.

My senses hyper-focus. Hands leave my wrist ties and no one speaks, all I hear is footsteps. Some rounding the desk, some in front of me. My pulse races with adrenaline and my needy sexy is throbbing.

"Look how wet she is for us, boys. Her thighs are glistening." Marco's husky voice fills the room. And someone groans in front of me. I am pretty sure it's Enzo.

"Please..." I whimper, sounding as needy as I feel.

The person in front of me strokes a thumb down my jaw and over my lips. "Always so needy for us..." Enzo groans.

"Please..." I whimper again.

I'm met with a sharp sting to my ass. "Ahhh!" I bellow and I'm met with another smack from something leather. The bite is worse and I think I love it.

"Now you're going to count how many times I spank this perfect little ass with my belt. That was one." Nic's voice is basically a growl with suppressed need.

Smack "Two."

Smack "Three."

My sex throbs worse than before and I feel myself getting more drenched with every smack.

Smack "Four."

Smack "Five."

The belt clatters to the floor and a strong body presses up against me, his body covering my back, his breathing in my ear.

Please fuck me, fuck me now and give me the best orgasm of my life!

NICHOLE STEEL

"You're such a needy little slut for us. We turned your ass into a strawberry, and you have a fucking river between your legs." Nic's gruff whisper has me fighting my restraints to push into his rock solid cock.

"I am only a slut for you," I mutter breathlessly

Nic slams into me all the way to the hilt.

"Ah! Yes Nic!" I bellow out in relief and an intoxicating mix of pleasure and pain.

He slams into me at a punishing pace, and I feel myself building.

He doesn't relent and I want more than anything to touch him, but these damn restraints won't let me.

I'm close now. The beautiful, boneless, oblivion is right there. My thighs start to quiver and I'm right on the edge..

The fucker pulls out!

"What Nic, No! Please!" I'm not above begging to come at this point. Every nerve ending is like a live wire and I'm desperate for relief.

"Enzo fill our brat's mouth up," Nico barks.

"Open up darling." Enzo taps my lips with his cock and I part my lips for him. I gag on his cock as he punishes my mouth, but I take all of him.

"I only allow good girls to come and you chose to be a brat tonight." Nic's gruff voice is in my ear.

"Marco punish her ass," Nic commands.

Cool lube drips on my ass. Fear and anticipation fill me. I see why I needed a safe word now. My body is being used and punished. This is so intense, and I desperately want to take all that they give to me.

Marco pushes into me slowly. "Relax Little Bird, you've got to let me in. Be a good girl and I might let you come."

I moan around Enzo's cock and they both groan.

Fuck, please let me come! Enzo's cock begins to twitch in my mouth and I swirl my tongue around his tip.

After three more thrusts, Enzo spills down my throat and like the needy slut I am for my boys, I suck every drop out and swallow him down.

"Shit, Sweet Peach!" Enzo groans in both pleasure and surprise. "You sucked me like a damn straw!"

Enzo leaves my front and I feel Nico's firm hand on my jaw. "Look at you taking all of our cocks. What do you think boys, has she redeemed herself? Should we let her come?"

They don't respond and my desperation overflows. I won't last with Marco's unrelenting pace.

"Please... I'm right fucking there."

"Marco, make her come," Nico orders

Marco's fingers find my sensitive bud, making sweet circles. "Come for me," he whispers and I soaring off the cliff into a climax that makes me see fucking stars.

Marco follows me with two more pumps, spilling into me. He pulls out and I'm exhausted from the earth moving orgasm I just had.

"You're not done yet," Nico barks "Untie her."

I feel the boys at my wrists in seconds, untying me with a gentleness not there earlier. They remove the blindfold and the light stings my eyes, but my heart swells when I see my boys.

As soon as I'm free, Nic's firm hands flip me onto my back and I stare up at him as he holds my legs in his firm grip.

"You. Are. Mine. You understand me?" His voice is commanding, but his eyes are claiming.

"Yes, Nic. I am yours. Ahhh!" I whimper as he pushes into me.

Nic's pace is softer this time. He is no longer punishing me, but loving me. Pleasure begins to build again, but this time I want to come with him.

Slowly I sit forward and wrap arms around his neck as he fucks me against his desk.

My thighs quiver as I pull him closer. I need all of him right here, right now.

With three more pumps he spills into me. "Fuck Chelsey!" he bellows and I follow him into another earth-shattering climax.

We stay still, enjoying the aftershocks in each other's embrace.

Slowly, he lifts my boneless body from the desk and lays me on a couch in the corner of the room.

"We should be close to closing by now. Stay with her and I'll wrap up out here," Nic's relaxed voice tells the boys.

"Don't got to tell me twice." Marco beams and I'm tucked into his arms as he joins me on the couch.

Nic kisses my forehead gently. "Rest, *Mio Tesoro*." And I slowly start to doze off. I hear the click of the door closing and know that he is gone.

Chapter 19
Nico

I just made love to Chesley Ryan. First I punished her and god damn was that really fucking satisfying after her acting like an innocent little brat all evening.

Then my brothers got into it and I think I enjoyed watching her take their demanding cocks just as much as giving her mine, but somewhere in the middle of all that I needed her. Needed to claim her, to let the feelings out.

She took it all, the beautiful and the ugly, and craved more. I gave her a safe word, because I didn't want to push her past her limits, but when it comes to us I don't know if she has any.

I should feel more relaxed but I'm more flustered than anything. Raking my hand through my hair I make my way to the bar. Everyone has cleared out for the evening and it's just staff clean up.

"Everything good boss?" Mark stares at me over his whiskey glass.

"Fine," is all I say as I scan the room and he huffs in return. My brain is too full of Chelsey to give him more of an answer and Mark is a man of little words.

Chelsey is our prisoner. She is with us because we picked her up and if she could leave safely, she might just fly away like the little bird Marco calls her.

The thought causes a pang in my chest. I shouldn't fucking care about her. She is here as a toy and the end game was always to send her packing. But now I don't know if I'll be the same if she goes.

"Boss. You're going to want to see this," Mark grumbles as he tosses back the last of his whiskey, sliding his phone down the bar to me.

What the fuck now...

There on the screen is our side building security camera showing David fucking Ryan talking to Reggie.

"Great, apparently old man David has a death wish. Tell Mitch to bring the car around then take the other guys and bring those two idiots in here."

Just another stupid fire for me to deal with. Marching back to my office I already feel tense enough to snap someone's neck. I know it's basically asking for a war by having Chelsey here, but nobody forces my hand. David was given his only warning and the other night my girl confirmed he had her raped. Repeatedly...

Barging into my office, Enzo and Marco are still cuddling and doting over a gorgeously passed out Chelsey, but as soon as their eyes meet mine they know something is up.

Enzo is on his feet and grabbing clothes in a second, closely followed by Marco. "What's going on?" Enzo's voice is all business.

"David Ryan appears to have never left Seattle and now is being brought in along with Reggie."

"Reggie is always involved in stupid shit." Marco is clearly annoyed as he throws on his clothes.

"So what are we doing with her?" Enzo nods at Chelsey and his face is pinched with concern. "It's risky to have her here with David."

"Mitch is pulling around the car. One of you boys will see her home safe-"

A knock on the door is followed Mark's voice, "Sir, the company you requested is in the lounge area waiting."

"Well I guess there goes the plan to get her out of here." My voice drips with the anger I feel. "With me now."

I roll my shoulders then open the door,. "Lock her in there and let's go." I nod breezing past Mark, my brothers close behind.

· • ● ● ● • ● ● ● • ·

Last time David was here, I promised death, and he was damn near shaking in his boots. This time is different. He holds himself confidently, wearing a cocky ass grin that I'm dying to knock off his face.

Reggie on the other hand appears like he may actually piss himself. The gang leader knows he fucked up big this time. But why was he with David in the first place.

They stand with my guys surrounding them, while my brothers and I take a seat in the lounge chairs. This is our house, our territory, and our muscle. We are the masters here, they are the peasants.

"Reggie, Reggie, Reggie. You got some mighty big balls to betray us," Marco's cool voice scolds him as he twirls a knife between his fingers.

While I oversee our business dealings, Marco oversees the gangs and drug dealers. Our hands are clean, but we can't stop them, so we keep them in check instead.

"Boss, I didn't!" Reggie shakes. "I swear, I would never betray you!"

"Well then how do you explain you meeting with this man here?" Marco points the tip of the knife at David. "You see he is an ally and known associate of our biggest rival and you're telling me you meeting with him isn't a betrayal?"

"Boss, I don't know anything! He got a hold of me a month ago about doing some digging on a woman named Chelsey Ryan." Reggie is downright panicked. "He needed to find her and offered me three grand!"

"So your life is only worth three grand? Got it."

"What! Boss No!" Reggie bellows, pleading with my brother.

"Take Reggie to the basement and get all the information he gathered on Chelsey Ryan. If he cooperates, let him walk away and prove his loyalty." Marco sneers. "But if you feel he is holding back, cut off fingers, and don't let him walk out of here alive unless you're sure he is to be trusted."

"Yes sir." Two of our guys grab Reggie, dragging him away.

We listen to Reggie beg and bellow until they're gone then my focus goes to David who still looks like a proud motherfucker.

"Get that smug look off your face before I knock it off you myself," I growl at him.

"David you were told to stay the hell out of our territory," Enzo chimes in beside me. "Yet here you are again? Care to explain yourself or do you prefer a bullet in the brain?"

Enzo knows how pissed off I am, and he is right to intervene. We need information and the look David is wearing has my stomach knotting, like he knows something we don't.

"No one will be killing me today." He stares right at me, practically begging me to do something.

"And why the fuck is that?" I growl at him.

"Oh well you see, my friend Reggie confirmed for me that my daughter was working at a club called Players about a month ago. She's in Seattle and Riccardo sent me here himself to fetch her." He steps forwards and Mark grabs his shoulder.

"You see, he has big plans for her. His wife appears to be barren, and he needs to continue his line. So, my darling daughter will give him lots of beautiful babies." He shrugs and tosses his hands to the side like this is of no consequence to him. "So if you kill me, Riccardo will come here looking for her himself and then you will have much larger problems."

My stomach rolls at the idea of Riccardo making her have his babies. Raping her every chance his gets. Her cries for him to stop. The images set my anger past its boiling point. David's acting like he has the trump card here, but all he is a rabid dog set loose to terrorize society.

I lunge from my chair and grab him around the throat. It would be so damn easy to snap his neck here and now.

"You think I'm scared of a war with Riccardo? Seattle is Romano territory and he wouldn't have the balls to fuck with me in my city," I growl squeezing harder.

David turns shades of red and purple, and I would love to watch the lights go out of his eyes right now. He is a pawn that had my girl raped and traumatized.

My brothers pulled me back.

"Mark, lock him in the basement cell until we can figure out what to do with him," Enzo orders and I shake them off me as Mark ushers him away.

My anger got the better of me, but no one will be getting anywhere near my girl except me and my brothers. Anyone who tries will fucking die and I will enjoy every minute of their death.

Chapter 20
Chelsey

All the lights are on in the office, but the boys are gone and my naked body is covered with a small blanket. It's surprising that they left me in here completely alone.

A small sense of worry fills my chest and I climb from the couch and go to the computer on Nic's desk. The time says it's four in the morning, so the club should be well closed. *Where the hell are my boys?*

Looking over the screen I see a small camera icon, that's hopefully the security cameras so I can find them.

Bingo! Relief hits me as the cameras load up, showing different areas of the club, but my stomach drops when I see them.

There are many men in the lounge area, most I don't recognize, but for sure that is my boys and my father.

Shit! No... no, no, no! Tears roll down my face. The time has come where I've outlived my usefulness and now they are sending me away.

What was shared just hours ago felt invigorating and intimate to me, but I guess I'm what I always was. Just a fuck toy.

My heart shatters and more tears fall as I watch the meeting unfold A deal is being made.

I will never escape now. I will be used and abused by Riccardo and his men until he tires of me and kills me. A room like this one will be all I see and there will be no choices or safe words.

Sobs wrack through my body and I drop to the floor hugging myself. It was stupid to think they cared about me, for me to develop feelings for them. I imagined a future with picnics, movie nights, games. *I was being stupid.*

I'm not sure how long I cry on the floor, but I cry until there are no tears left.

The lock on the door clicks open and the door slides open.

Heartbreak and sadness give way to panic. I would rather die than go with my father. There is more dignity in death here and now than at the hands of that monster disguised as a man.

"Little Bird, are you okay?" Marco's concern is etched all over him as I spring from the floor and rush to the couch.

His body is relaxed, but his face is pinched with worry as he walks towards me, his hand stretched out.

"Fuck you," I growl at him while tears spill down my cheeks again. I need to stuff this shit down. It's only showing them my weakness. I move around the room grabbing my clothes, never taking my eyes off him.

"Excuse me?" He sounds baffled. "Chelsey, what's going on?" He takes another step towards me.

"Don't take another fucking step, Marco!" I shout getting dressed, and he freezes in his tracks.

I'm almost completely dressed when Enzo and Nico walk into the room. Their muscles tense and their eyebrows pinch in confusion.

"What's going on?" Enzo asks, looking at Marco, then turning to face me. "Are you hurt?" his voice raises an octave as he starts towards me and I back myself up to the wall away from him.

He stops in his tracks. "Don't come any closer to me, asshole!" I shout at him, angry tears dripping down my cheeks.

"Chelsey, I'm sorry if we hurt you earlier. We gave you a safe word so we wouldn't go past your limit," Nico gruff voice barks behind his brothers.

"You think this is about earlier? You all fucking me over that desk was perfect. But how low do you have to be to fuck someone and then hours later hand them over to their worst nightmare!"

"Excuse me? We're not handing you over to anyone." Enzo sounds so convincing, but I saw them. All three of them in that meeting with my father.

"Bullshit. I would rather die than leave this room with you three. I fucking saw you on the cameras with my father!"

"Sweet Peach, We are protecting you—"

"Oh I'm sure you think you are! After I turned eighteen, my father forced me to fuck his men! He had me raped almost daily until I ran away, I never had a fucking choice! Then I met you three, you made me feel freedoms I never had before. You made me open my heart to you, and then you go and betray me to the man of my nightmares! If you think I am going anywhere with you willingly, you have another thing coming," I growl completely dressed in my napkin of an outfit.

I am geared up to fight, to run, to do whatever it takes to escape.

"Damn it, Chelsey! Listen to us!" Nico's voice booms with frustration. "We are protecting you from David. Let's get back to the apartment and we will explain everything."

"Fuck off, Nico. I told you about my father having me raped and you still brought him here. You're no better than he is."

"We don't have time for this here. Let's go boys," Nico orders.

Next thing I know Enzo and Marco are grabbing me. Screaming at the top of my lungs, I head butt Marco in the face hard enough his nose is spitting blood.

"Fuck!" he bellows

Turing I stomp on Enzo's foot and he winces. Distracted, I turn my face and bite his shoulder until I taste the rusty tang of blood.

"Damn it, Chelsey!" he shouts.

I didn't survive my father just because of my looks and now these boys will learn that the hard way.

From behind a cloth and strong hand covers my nose and mouth. Damn it no... Everything starts to feel heavy, my eyes heavy. Chloroform... Rookie mistake not to look for the third guy.

I'm done. I will be given to Riccardo and my greatest fear will come to pass. The worst part is that it's happening from the men I let myself fall in love with...

Chapter 21
Marco

S he felt betrayed. That much was obvious. She couldn't contain the broken-hearted tears streaming down her face and right now all I care about is fixing this with her. She's out cold in her bed with her head in my lap as I twirl her hair in my fingers. She looks so peaceful with her eyes gently shut and her face relaxed.

NICHOLE STEEL

Enzo is a wreck next to me staring at her hand in his. Body rigid, his eyebrows are pinched together, and every few seconds he rubs his thumb over the back of her hand like he is trying to sooth both of them. Meanwhile Nic sits at the end of the bed staring at the floor like a statue. The only movement he has done over the past fifteen minutes since we got here is breathe.

She has become a piece of all of us and we are all aching from what just went down. She didn't trust us, she did believe us, and she confirmed our suspicions of her never having a choice in her sex life. This night went from perfect to all around messed up in thirty seconds flat.

"You didn't have to use chloroform on her," Enzo grumbles, still staring at her hand.

"What else did you want me to do?" Nic shrugs. "She wasn't going to come easy. Your bruised shoulder and Marco's busted nose is proof of that, and if she kept screaming at us we risked David hearing her."

"I don't know man. I just hate this!" Enzo damn near whimpers "I feel helpless waiting for her to wake up."

We are not soft men. Enzo is the softest of us, but to whimper... She really must be his whole damn heart.

"She's going to be fine. She'll wake up in another hour or so," I reassure my brother.

"Yeah but in what kind of state? You saw her, Marco. She was heartbroken, betrayed. Scared for her life. How do we fix that?"

No one responds. It's the question we are all asking. What happens when she wakes up? My chest throbs the more I think about it, but I know the solution.

"We give her a choice." My brothers turn to me. "Offer for her to leave us and go live her life. Offer her protection while she's in Seattle to the best of our abilities. But give her the only things she has ever wanted. The choice and her freedom."

As soon as the words leave my lips, I feel ready to fall into a million pieces. Chelsey was supposed to be nothing but a toy, but somehow she filled a hole in our hearts we didn't even know we were missing.

"What about David?" Nico growls. "He is not going to just let her go and if we kill him, Riccardo will come. We can't protect her from Riccardo if she's not with us."

"Are you suggesting we let that fucker walk?!" Enzo yells. "He's a sick bastard who not only planned to sell her but also had her raped almost daily since her eighteenth birthday! That fucker will die by either your hand or mine, but either way he is not fucking walking!"

Enzo has a fire in his eyes and I'm willing to wager that when it comes to David, that is a piece of what he is holding in.

My rage on the other hand is under a tight lock and key. Specifically reserved to give David the longest, and most painful death I can come up with. But Nico is right, we have to let him walk if we are going to give Chelsey a choice.

"What if we use Reggie?" I ask. "We could have him pass information that Chelsey has moved on to California. David will leave town in pursuit and then Chelsey can be safe here in Seattle."

"Yeah. Until she's not! The only safe place for her is here with us!" Enzo is breaking before our eyes. His eyes are puffy like the idea of her leaving might actually make him cry and the pure emotion in his voice makes my own aching heart hurt worse than it already is.

"Enzo, Marco's right," Nic sighs. "We'll send David packing with false information, and then we'll give Chelsey the freedom she has desperately wanted her whole life." His voice is raw, he hasn't shown his emotions like this since our parents died. "We all love her. But it's because we love her that we must sacrifice for her. We will bear this pain so she can finally let go of hers."

Nico shifts on the bed and grabs Chelsey's feet staring directly at her peaceful face. "*Mio Tesoro*, I love you with every inch of the heart I thought died years ago. You broke through my walls and loved every dark corner of me." A single tear spills down his face as he pours out his heart to our girl. "You never took my shit laying down but met it with your own fire. *Mio Tesoro*, you are a piece of me now and even though you are going to leave, you will always hold my heart."

Chapter 22
Enzo

"Where's the big scary dog?" David mocks as the door to our basement cell closes behind Mark and I.

"None of your damn business. I'm here. You'll be dealing with me." My voice is stern, a almost a growl. Though David looks just as smug as he did when we first dealt with him this morning, relaxed back in a folding metal chair with his hands behind his head and feet kicked out.

If it wasn't for the safety of my girl I would skin him alive here and now. And thoroughly enjoy his screams, his begging for mercy that would never be given.

"You boys are all so up tight. I think you need to relax more," David muses.

"Fuck off David. If it were up to me I would kill you here and now for not leaving our territory when told to. But my brother would like to send a gesture of good will to Riccardo. So, we're letting you go."

"If you think I'm leaving this city when my daughter is here, you're sorely mistaken." He sits up in the chair, leaning forward on his elbows almost like he is gearing up to fight me. Little does he know he's playing right into our hands.

"That's part of the good gesture. Follow your daughter's trail until you find her, but while you are in Seattle our men will be assisting in your endeavors."

"Fine, whatever helps you sleep at night, pretty boy." David stands and chews like he has gum in his mouth. *Please*

Lord above keep me from kicking the crap out of this man! "So, if you're done wasting my time, I'm leaving now."

He walks straight to Mark and Mark looks to me for permission to open the door. I nod my approval and David walks right out, like a man in a police station walking out knowing they just got away with a crime.

Rubbing my temples, I sit down in the folding chair David was in moments ago. How the fuck did life go from feeling perfect to the biggest shit storm in mere hours! I don't know if I need to beat the shit out of somebody, drown myself in a bottle of tequila, or hide away and fucking cry like a baby.

Checking my phone there is a new text from Marco and nothing from Nico. Nico stayed home with Chelsey and Marco went to deal with Reggie. In hindsight, leaving Nico home with our girl might not have been the best idea since she is definitely geared up for a fight, but when we left she was still passed out.

> Marco: Everything is set with Reggie. He will contact David this evening.

> Me: Ok. David was released about 10min ago.

> Marco: Fuck…. We are actually doing this.

No shit we are actually doing this. It was his stupid ass idea! I get that she needs her freedom, but I just wish there was another way so I wasn't fucking shattered. And this is only a taste, it will be so much worse when she is actually gone.

"Boss…" Mark drones from the cell door.

"What?"

"David Ryan has officially left and is headed to Players as we speak."

"Great. I guess, let's get back to the apartment."

Chapter 23
Chelsey

"**N**IC! LET ME THE HELL OUT OF HERE!" I scream banging on the door. If I was the size of one of the guys I would have broken the stupid thing down by now.

I've been locked in my room for probably close to an hour now and my fist hurts from how much I've hit this door.

At first I woke up in my bed groggy as hell with Nico sitting on the end. Then I remembered the sex, the betrayal, the fight. Nico using the chloroform on me! Fucking bastard drugged me!

When I threw the flower vase at his head from my dresser he left saying, "When the guys get back and you calm down, we will talk." Then locked me in this room.

There's really nothing to talk about. They stole my heart, and are returning me to my worst nightmare. Like it was some sick twisted game to them! I'll never win against these guys plus all the extra men everyone in this world has, but I won't go without a fight. They need to see what they have truly done here and I hope they fucking bleed for it!

Relinquishing the fight for now, I slump on the floor against the wall. My breathing is labored, my throat raw from the yelling, plus I think my hand may be bruised. It's already turning a purplish color.

I can't believe I let myself think I was worth more than my body. How could I have been so dumb to allow myself to want them and worse harbor feelings for them. Even now as my anger gives way to sadness, I find myself longing for my

Zo's sweet care and Marco's firm cuddle. Nic's safety. Stupid, Stupid, Stupid....

I can't hold back the tears as they silently fall down my face and I bring my knees to my chest, simply to hold myself.

I have felt a lot of pain in my life. My father murdered my mother, my step-mother hated me, I was toughened up by being a drug runner, and then became a sexual servant. But the betrayal of the men I love, the men that finally felt like safety and home, that cuts deeper than anything else.

"Sweet Peach...We're all here. Can we come in and talk to you?" Enzo's voice is such a soothing comfort to my aching heart. But my heart really needs to catch up to the fact we cannot love him anymore. He is a monster just like any other man on planet Earth.

"Sure. Not like I have a choice in the matter," I shout through the door and bat away my tears before moving to the bed to sit down. They will not see my hurt and my weakness. Not after what they have done.

Slowly they come into the room and each one surveys me.

Marco moves towards me half rushed. His eyes are scowled and sad, with nothing but concern in his features.

I know I should have moved away, but my heart has not quite gotten with the program yet.

Lifting my hand, he frowns as he inspects the bruised knuckles. "Chelsey darling, did you do this to yourself?" His voice is laced with sadness and a hint of anger, but not towards me.

"Of course I did. I was trying to get out of this room since Nic locked me in here!" I turn and pin him with my eyes.

"I wouldn't have locked you in here if you could have been civil and not thrown a vase at my head!" Nic shouts, allowing my anger to bloom once again like a rose in spring.

"Okay that is enough!" Enzo shouts. "Chelsey we are not giving you to David or Riccardo. We are giving you your freedom. So please just listen to us for one damn minute!"

It feels like all the air was sucked out of the room and my fight vanishes as I digest his words. *They're giving me my freedom.*

Sitting back a little on the bed, my shoulder relaxes a fraction and I face Enzo. "Okay, I'm listening..." It comes out hoarse and breathless.

"David came to Seattle looking for you a while back," Enzo sighs. "We thought Nic and Marco sent him packing, but last night we found him meeting with a local drug dealer. We brought him in to find out what he knew about your whereabouts." Panic rises in my chest. How can they give me my freedom if my dad knows I am here? "I gave the drug dealer specific instructions to give David bullshit intel that should lead him to California. We have a tail on your dad to be sure he actually follows it."

This is so much to process. My father showed up here again, and they didn't hand me over but protected me. Again.

"I am such an idiot." Tears well in my eyes. I caused my boys so much pain and for what? They did nothing but love and protect me. "I am so sorry." My chin wobbles at the words as the guilt hits my chest. "I busted your nose, I bit your shoulder, and I threw a vase at you. All because you were taking care of me." Tears fall.

All three surround me. Marco and Enzo on either side of me and Nic sits behind me.

Nic pulls me back to his chest, while Marco gives me a shoulder to lean on and Zo wipes my tears away.

My men take care of me. They claimed me. I am theirs and I was so stupid to think otherwise.

"Chelsey, you're okay," Enzo soothes. "You have had to fight to protect yourself most of your life. You felt betrayed and in danger. It was a natural response to fight us. Don't feel bad."

My boys allow me to process everything in silence for a few minutes.

"Little Bird, we were serious about giving you your freedom." Marco's voice is downcast and sadness is his eyes. "You have wanted freedom to choose your own path and future for as long as we have known you and I'm assuming it's been a lifelong desire for you."

I nod my head to confirm what he is saying, but I don't have the words to speak.

"We have everything set for you. Once your dad leaves town, Mark will be head of your security." Marco's eyes are red and puff like he is holding back tears and I'm completely speechless. "We'll be paying him but you will be his boss. He will protect you until Riccardo loses interest in you. We arranged a small apartment for you downtown and set aside plenty of cash for you to live off of." He tries to smile, but it's half-hearted at best. "You will be free to fly my Little Bird and you won't have to see any of us again."

I've wanted this my whole life, but is it still what I want?

My heart aches at the idea of leaving the guys, but there is a whole world out there. As much as it pains me, I think I have to leave. I need to find out what it's like to be free.

Chapter 24
Nico

A few days have passed and Chelsey has been awkward around us ever since. I think she has been trying to create distance, but it's fucking miserable.

We got word yesterday that David left Seattle and Chelsey spent the evening packing. Meanwhile I didn't get a wink of sleep, working all evening to keep her out of my mind.

Her leaving is fucking killing me and she doesn't even know it because I refuse to tell her. But this is a good thing for her, this is what she needs. So, I will bear this pain. I can't burden her with my love.

"Nic…" Her soft voice flows into my office, startling me. "I'm all packed and Mark is in the kitchen waiting. I um… I just wanted to say goodbye and thank you." She fidgets nervously with her simple knee length blue dress. It's tight on her torso, but has a full skirt and she looks absolutely stunning in it.

Of course, Mio Tesoro. I will do anything and be anything for you. I love you now and I will love you forever. You hold my heart, now go find the world.

Standing from my chair I cross my office to her. "Take care of yourself and listen to Mark." It comes out stern like I'm ordering her, but I can't be soft. It will hurt too much.

Pulling a flip cell phone from my pocket I grab her hand and slap it into it. "This is for you. You don't have to use it and we will not contact you on it. It only has four numbers in it. Mine, Enzo's, Marco's, and Mark's. If you need anything, use it."

Her face is downcast, her mouth is set into a flatline. This should be an exciting day for her, but instead she is upset. Probably from my stupid asshole self.

"Come on *Mio Tesoro*." I grab her hand lead her to the kitchen.

"Nic, what does *Mio Tesoro* mean?" Even her voice is downcast.

"It doesn't matter now," I say just before entering the full kitchen.

Marco, Enzo, and Mark are waiting for the woman of the hour. Enzo comes rushing towards her, wrapping her in a hug, lifting her off her feet. I can't help but roll my eyes, always the bleeding heart.

"Enjoy your freedom, Sweet Peach, and if you need me, never hesitate to call me okay?" His voice is so soft, damn near musical.

"Okay Zo, I won't hesitate." She offers him a pained half smile before turning to Marco.

Marco saunters over to us and grabs her chin with his finger and thumb. "No sadness, this is a happy day. I'm going to miss you Little Bird, but go find the world."

She nods at him and bats away a stray tear she lets fall then walks to Mark. The elevator pings open and my stomach twists in knots. I want to yell at her not to leave us. To tell her that she made me, made us whole.

She enters the elevator and turns to face us. "Thank you, all of you for everything. I will miss you." The elevator closes, and just like that my heart dies once more.

We stand in the kitchen for what feels like an eternity. I keep hoping the elevator will come back up and she will be here, but I know it will never actually happen.

"Boys you got shit to do, now go do it and quit moping in the kitchen," I bark at them. "We always knew she was temporary."

"Seriously Nic?" Marco yells. "You know this became so much more than just her being a fucking plaything."

"We all got attached and now she's gone and never coming back. The sooner we move on the better. Now go get your shit done." I yell back like a stern father.

"Whatever you say, heartless fucking bastard." Marco is picking a fight as he scowls at me getting into my space. "Did you even actually care about her?"

"I am not going to do this with you," I growl at him.

"Bro you going to get in on this or no?" He turns to Enzo whose eyes still have not left the elevator.

"You two do what you want. Kill each other for all I care," he says sternly turning from the elevator before shoving past us out of the kitchen.

"You know what Nic you're not worth it right now. Go back to your little hole of an office and just leave me the hell alone." Marco shoves past me.

We are all broken, that much is obvious. But how the hell are we going to recover? No matter how we manage, we will never be the same.

Chapter 25
Marco

The club tonight is at max capacity, which is great for business, but shitty for me since one of bartenders called out sick. I've been behind the bar helping sling drinks for close to three hours and we're just starting to catch up. Next time, Enzo is coming back here, and I'll work the floor.

"Mary, you good back here?" I yell to one of the bartenders.

"Yeah, I'll page you on the radio if it gets out of control again." She turns to pour a beer and I move to walk the upper floor. Really it's just an excuse to get away from all the people.

It's been two weeks, but I can't stand to be here or around my brothers. I shouldn't blame anyone but myself for her leaving, but even though it broke me, I hope it made her whole.

"Situation out front, requesting additional support," Mitch's voice fills my earpiece and something like excitement fills me. *Time to go fuck up some frat boys.*

"On my way," I radio back

"Marco, back to the bar. I'll help Mitch," Nic's voice comes over the radio, but I don't give a fuck what he wants right now. He wants extra help at the bar, he can do it himself.

I walk through the club, and different girls eye me like I'm candy, but I couldn't care less. There's only one girl I want, and she's never coming back.

Nic beats me to the door and scowls deep when he sees me. "I said man the bar Marco." "Yeah, well, I don't really care. Now move, so I can see what Mitch needs."

A growl rumbles in his chest, as he clenches his fists at his side. I came to hopefully kick the asses of some out of line college kids, but my brother's face will work just as well.

"For once, just do as you're told," he barks, and that is all I need. I swing high and nail him right in the jaw. He turns beat red with anger, and tackles me to the ground, landing a blow of his own to my cheek.

"Enough you two!" Mitch yells, pulling Nic off me. "Now, what ever the fuck is going on you two need to work it out! This shit has gone on long enough."

Nic shoves from his grip and storms off and Mitch turns to me.

"Mark is gone with Chelsey." My chest pangs at the sound of her name. "You three need to get back to normal and give this security team the support we need."

I rub my hand over my jaw. "Yeah I know."

"I don't think you do." He crosses his arms over his chest. "One day, trouble will come again and if you three aren't back to normal, it could cost you your lives. Now, I don't care if it takes fucking a hundred bitches to get you there, just fix yourself before it's too late."

Mitch walks away and I look around at the gawking crowd.

I wish fucking a hundred women would fix this, but when I see my brothers, I see the men whose hearts ache for the same woman mine does. Time heals all wounds, but I doubt it can heal this one.

Chapter 26
Chelsey

D amn it, why does it always rain so much in Seattle? Here I am enjoying my mocha latte sitting on the park bench reading a book and now it has to start raining.

I've come to this little park almost daily since leaving a month ago. It's only about two blocks from my apartment, the same park *our* date was. I feel them here...

"Miss, can I offer you an umbrella?" Mark is always so attentive. He started as my security, but I like to think we have become friends.

"Sure, thanks Mark." I stand taking it from him and my eyes look over the park. Memories of Marco's strong arms holding me wash over me and I close my eyes basking in it, if only for a moment.

The ache in my chest is still just as fresh as the day I left. I miss them more than I've ever missed another person in my life. Umbrella in hand, I head to the pond.

I want to feel all of them.

The pond comes into view, and it looks dull and sad with the gray sky above and the drops of water hitting the surface. Enzo's voice fills my mind, *"I wanted to share my place with you and we all wanted to show you exactly what you mean to us,"* and tears threaten to spill from my eyes.

"Maybe we should just head back to the apartment." My voice is barely above a whisper as I try to contain the emotions threatening to flow from me.

"Yeah, that is probably for the best." Mark nods, empathy in his eyes. He allows me to lead the way.

Mark surveys our surroundings as we walk, even in an empty park. He can't relax because Riccardo is still out there. I just wish he could enjoy an outing too. But the fact is, I will never be truly safe until Riccardo is no longer a threat.

I pause when I realize where we are. The tree. The one where everything changed for Nic and I. Images flash through my mind and my heart breaks into pieces.

I thought by now it would be easy being away from them. I love everything about my newfound freedom except wishing they were here to share it with me.

This is what normal peoples lives are supposed to be like. Going to the grocery store, hanging out at the park, cleaning, going to the movies, meeting up with Slim for coffee. I even go hiking now. But instead of looking over my shoulder every ten seconds for men who might take me, now I look hoping to see my men there.

We reach the sidewalk outside the park, the raindrops forming puddles, but I'm lost in my thoughts. It would be so sexy to play with Marco in the rain. His white shirt would be sculpted to his chest, rain drops dripping down his smoldering face, I'm damn near panting at the thought as heat floods my core. Fuck I want my boys back...

Mark's phone rings and my attention immediately snaps to him. We freeze. His eyebrows knit together and his mouth sets into a line when he sees the name on the screen. My heart skitters at the idea that it's one of them.

"Yes," he answers in his flat firm tone. The longing in my heart has me wanting to reach out and take the phone. To hear their voice, to feel any sort of connection to them. *This truly is getting ridiculous Chelsey...*

"Currently I'm out, but when I get back to the apartment I will send over the report."

"Mark, is it one of the guys?" I scowl at him.

This is it Chelsey, you're officially desperate. Maybe even pathetic that you're stalking your bodyguard's phone.

Mark won't meet my gaze.

"Mark answer me," I half yell. "They pay your bill but I'm your boss, remember." I deepen my voice to a threatening growl, but to a man like Mark I am sure it sounds like a chihuahua growling at a German Shepard. But Mark meets my eyes and nods a slow yes.

My pulse skyrockets a hundred fold and my mind starts racing. *Are they checking on me? Do they miss me as much as I do them? Are they okay? Is someone hurt? Is my dad or Riccardo coming around again? Are they leaving town to deal with something?*

Shaking my head, I take off down the street. This is too much, too overwhelming. I have been fighting these feelings since the day I left and I can't anymore. I have to do something with my body, or I may actually explode. I ditch my umbrella, coffee, and book on the sidewalk, I just need to run!

"Fuck! Chelsey! I'll call you back," Mark yells into the phone.

Honestly I have no idea where I am running too, I am just running to escape the thoughts, the fears, the damn longing that won't leave.

Mark is closing in, but if he catches me will he stop me? I can't stop. Not until I feel like I can breathe. I veer left into an alleyway and then onto the main strip, flooded with people and umbrellas.

He won't be able to find me, but I don't care. I run through the people, dodging them until another alleyway appears. I take it and now Mark is gone completely. I am alone in the big city, and all I feel is overwhelmed!.

Run Chelsey. Run from your past. Run from the feelings. Run from the pain. Run from your security. Damn it Chelsey, you even ran from the men you love!

Tears spill down my cheeks and my chest aches, but I don't know if it's from my heart or my labored breathing.

When I can't run anymore, I hunch over and vomit into the sewer. My lungs burn and my legs quake, but I welcome the physical pain. It's better than the emotional.

Lifting my face, I see their building "Fucking hell, Chelsey."

I stand there unable to breathe as onlookers are staring at me with pity in their eyes. "Go to hell Karen!" I yell at some lady who begins to approach me, and she scurry's off like a wounded animal. I'm sure I look like a damsel in distress panting, holding my aching sides, and drenched to the bone.

Fuck this. Fuck this freedom that feels awful. Fuck running away from everything. And fuck them for making me feel like I had to leave.

Sopping wet and looking half homeless I march into their building. Mitch is at the counter and stands when he sees me. "Mrs. Ryan are you—"

"Not now!" I yell at him as I punch in the code to the elevator.

I'm not sure if this is pathetic desperation, anger, love, or maybe all three. But I don't want to be free if it means they are not with me.

The elevator door opens to an apartment that is totally silent. I take a seat in the breakfast nook on the other side of the kitchen. I don't care if I have to wait here in my sopping wet clothes all night, I will see them and tell them everything.

Thankfully, I don't have to wait long. The door dings open and

"Chelsey!" Nic's voice floods the kitchen. It's firm, angry, unwavering, and it feels like the first sunlight I've seen in weeks. "I'm right here." I stand with a squish of my clothes crossing my arms over my chest.

They look like a fresh breath of air even though they are all sweating, tense, and have looks of pure shock.

"Chelsey what the fuck!" Nico booms with anger. "You had us scared out of our minds, not to mention—"

"Nic that is enough!" I yell back and he shuts his mouth. That's a first, but good it's my turn to say what I have to say.

"I ran here because I'm tired of running okay."

Their eyebrows furrowed, and my sweet Zo even cocks his head a little to the side trying to figure out my meaning.

"I don't want to run from this. I have chosen very little in my life and you gave me my freedom. But damn it boys I want it with all of us!" I'm still yelling, but something inside is breaking. I move towards them, taking in every inch of them. "This is what feels like home and the whole time I was without you, all I wanted was this! What the hell is the point of having my freedom, when the men I want to be free with are not with me."

Saying it out loud is like a flood gate has opened. I am no longer speaking words, I'm spilling my heart and all the love I hold for them.

My voice softens, the fight starting to leave me. "Nic you are a broody, territorial asshole, but you love deeply and protect fiercely."

I look to Marco. "Marco, you are sunshine on a cloudy day. You make me laugh and always have some crazy idea in mind. You sacrifice for me, even when it's the worst thing for you."

And lastly Zo. "Enzo, you care deeper than the damn ocean and you would go to the ends of the earth if that is what someone you loved needed."

I take a step back, looking at my boys.

"I love you all for it! You claimed me as a plaything the night at Players, but here and now I want you to claim me as yours! Not as a plaything, but as a piece of you to love and build a life with." My voice definitely sounds desperate but I don't care.

"If you don't share my feelings tell me now and I'll let you go, but if you do, claim me now, because the saying if you love something set it free is the dumbest thing on planet Earth." I stand there staring at my beautiful boys.

Nic has his eyes down cast, muscles taught, jaw set, like he is fighting a war in himself. Marco looks like he just found his favorite toy. His eyes are bright, he is bouncing on his toes, and

NICHOLE STEEL

a smile is growing across his face. My sweet Zo's face is making my heart swell. The sheer love in his eyes...

He shoves past his brothers and wraps his strong arms around me, kissing me deeply. *This... this is what I have been needing.* I melt into him and part my lips for him to invade me. The kiss is tender, both of us pouring all of our love into it.

He pulls away and rests his forehead on mine. "I've missed you, my Sweet Peach..." His voice is like the sweetest of melody's.

"Alright, Enzo release the girl," Nic chastises in his deep brooding tone.

Enzo moves away and I already long for his touch. I cross my arms protectively over my chest. *I can take this, I can take the rejection Nico is about to give me...*

"Chelsey, you realize if we claim you now, you will be ours forever and we'll never let you go right?"

I wish his voice was sweet, but it's deep and commanding, and it makes me want to buckle at the knees.

"Yes..." I whisper, looking at the floor. I want to beg, but I don't want to stay out of pity either.

"And you want this?" he questions

"More than anything." *Please...*

Within a second, I am being lifted in the air by Nic and his mouth comes crashing down on mine with pure need. He steals my breath, and there is no breathing during this kiss.

The kiss breaks and Nic is already hauling me down the hall to the bedroom. "*Mio Tesoro*, you are fucking ours now and forever," he growls, and my heart swells.

"Sweet Little Bird, if you fly away from me again, I may actually die," Marco says next to me and when I turn to look at him, he claims me with a kiss, causing Nic to stop walking.

Enzo smiles at me. "You're Chelsey Romano now, Sweet Peach." Enzo jokes behind me and with that last statement I'm claimed now and forever by my amazing, perfect men.

Chapter 27
Enzo

My girl is back. She's fucking back! I've been a shell since she left. Just going through the motions of working the bar, cooking at home, and jerking off to the memory of her. Nic and Marco have been on the brink of killing each other, but with her back, she will make us whole again. She's our missing piece.

We have all been parched for her since she left. Even Marco the playboy, has been rejecting women. None of us have gotten laid since we had her bent over the desk in Nico's office.

Nic tosses her on her bed with a thump and she squeals.

My dick jumps at that sweet little sound. Chelsey fucking Romano, my Sweet Peach. First we claimed her and now she has claimed us.

Shoving past my brothers, I climb over her ready to take her as mine. Nic growls at me like the territorial ass he is, but I don't care.

I hover over her and drink in her emerald eyes, her thick pillow soft lips, her wet blond hair lying around her.

"Oh Sweet Peach, you will never know how much I missed you." I kiss her deeply.

"I fucking love you..." I groan against her lips.

"I love you, Zo..." She moans, arching her hips into mine.

Momentarily appeased, I roll to her side and begin pulling up her shirt to find her perfectly large tits.

Nic is quick to take my place. He grabs her by the throat and stares down at her with a tormenting smile.

"No safe word *Mio Tesoro*. You are going to take all of us at the same time."

Chelsey sucks in her bottom lip and presses deeper into my touch, never breaking eye contact with Nico.

"You are going to take us like a good girl because you were fucking made for us," he growls before crashing his lips into hers with such veracity it could be bruising.

My cock is hard as steel watching the two of them and I cannot wait to feel her around it.

Marco must be thinking the same thing, he is already naked and stroking himself on the other side of her.

Nic and Chelsey break apart, and Nic climbs off the bed, peeling off his clothes.

"My turn Little Bird," Marco coos at her and she instantly rolls on top of him.

She runs her hands over his sculpted chest and there is a pang of jealousy in my gut, but I know my time is coming.

Chelsey kisses him and I reach over pulling her hips to the side. I make quick work of removing the last of her clothes. Her pussy is already glistening with need, that I am desperate for a taste of.

Marco and her break apart and I grab her hips, pulling her to sit on my face. She lets out a moan, and I work her clit like the expert I am.

"Fuck Zo, you do that so well..." she whimpers as I make intoxicating circles over her swollen bud and suck it into my mouth, tasting her incredible sweetness.

"Be a good girl and suck my cock while you come on my brothers face," Nic orders in a deep husky tone and instantly I feel her body start bobbing on him.

Nic groans and Chelsey's legs start to quiver as she squeezes my face with her thighs.

"Fuck.... Chelsey you look so good with my cock in your mouth," Nic groans.

She's close, so I slide two fingers into her entrance and begin pumping along with the sweet circles my tongue makes on her clit.

Three pumps in she explodes for me and I hear her mewling around my brother's cock.

My cock is straining so hard against my pants right now, it may snap off if I don't do something.

Chelsey moves from my face and I stand and get rid of these fucking pants.

"Come here *Mio Tesoro*, I want to feel that pussy around my cock."

Chelsey slides onto my brother, moaning with every inch she takes. What a fucking sight to behold.

Nic sits forward holding her still as he sucks one of her hard peaks into his mouth, teasing the other with his hand.

"Ah... Nic... I love you..." she whimpers with her cries of pleasure.

"And I love you, *Mio Tesoro*." He lays back, grabs her hips, and thrusts with such force she cries out.

"Nic what does my name mean?" she asks breathlessly has he pumps into her.

"My treasure. You're my fucking treasure," he growls.

I slide up behind her and caress her breasts and she leans into my touch. "You ready to take another one, Sweet Peach?"

"Mm-hm," she moans.

Nic stops moving and holds her hips for me. I drip some lube over her dark hole and press myself in.

"Oh God..." she bellows as I fill her inch by inch.

Marco slides up next to her and grabs her face, pulling her attention to him. He kisses her deeply. "You're doing great, Little Bird. Now open that perfect mouth for me."

She does so without hesitation. Now that I am fully seated in her, I nod to my brother and all three of us begin to work her.

She feels better than I remember, maybe because I know I never have to let her go. It only takes a few seconds for her walls to quake and she goes soaring into another orgasm.

"Ahh... Guys... I love you!" she cries out, gripping me like a fucking vice. It's incredible...

We work her through her orgasm, my own release building as my spine begins to tingle.

Marco grunts his release and Chelsey swallows him down. He leans over kissing her as Nic bellows his own release. "Shit, *Mio Tesoro*..."

Her walls quiver once more and Marco reaches down to start playing with her clit.

"Come for us one more time Little Bird."

"Oh Shit!" She falls over the edge again and I follow.

"Wow, Sweet Peach. You are perfect," I whisper. "Nic's right, you are made for us."

We all drink her in as we lay down on the large bed together. Chelsey is snuggled into Nic's chest, which is surprising because he doesn't cuddle. Marco is pressed against her backside, holding her hips. I find my space at the end of the bed holding her feet.

Not the best spot, but Nic needs this cuddle more than I do at the moment.

She is fucking ours, now and forever. I don't know what my brothers will want the future to look like, but I could see us in a house with a yard and maybe a dog. I never considered bringing a child into the world, but here I sit questioning if she wants children. If she does, my brothers and I are damn well going to give them to her.

We're all willing to cater to her every desire and need, and we'd die before we let anything happen to her.

Chapter 28
Chelsey

A week has passed since I came back and I don't think the guys and I have left the bed much since. We certainly haven't left the apartment.

We're all kind of on this high and I can't believe this is my life now. Sitting in the little breakfast nook, I pretend to read a silly romance novel, but really I'm ogling a shirtless

Marco while he cooks pancakes, with bacon, and toast, per my request.

Nic is in his office trying to catch up on some work, and Enzo decided to hit the gym. I made a joke about keeping him in shape and responded with, "I have to work out to keep up with you, my needy little Peach." A smile crosses my face at the memory.

"Good part of the book, Little Bird?" Marco asks, sliding in next to me and putting an arm around my waist.

"Yeah it's pretty good." I turn and smile at him. Lies, all lies. With Marcos bare chest and chiseled abs right in front of me, how could I ever focus on a book.

"Really? What's your favorite part so far?" He raises an eyebrow at me. *Shit.*

"Umm well if you must know it's the sweet bar scene that just finished," I say matter-of-factly.

Marco tilts my book to see the cover, it's a historical romance based in the 1700s.

Marco laughs loudly. "I caught you Little Bird. You weren't reading at all."

"I was trying to, but it's difficult to focus on a book when my real life book boyfriend is standing shirtless in the kitchen!" I try to justify myself, but I seem to just be digging the hole deeper as Marco's grin doubles in size.

"You know if you were ogling me, you should have just said so. Now I am going to have to punish that mouth of yours for lying to me," he growls in my ear.

Anticipation swirls in my belly, heat searing between my thighs. I honestly don't think I will ever get enough of these guys. *My guys.*

Some girls are blessed with a great man, a nice house, and an everyday fairytale. But somehow I managed to be blessed with three amazing, unique, perfect men. I didn't get an everyday fairytale. No, I got something so rare that it's the happily ever after bedtime story level fairytale.

"No fucking in the kitchen you two," Nic barks as he comes into the kitchen and begins fixing a breakfast plate.

A devilish smile forms on my face, because cranky Nic is fun in bed. The punishments are great, but the love and orgasms are better.

"Yes sir..." I purr at him and his eyes instantly shoot to mine. Submissive, bratty Chelsey is always a sure-fire way to get Nic going.

"Chelsey, no," he commands, and it makes me want to double down. "We have important things to attend to today."

Great, I guess our happy uninterrupted bubble of sex, love, and happiness, is finally going to pop.

"Ugh. I guess work can't wait forever." Marco grumbles, kisses me quickly, and jumps out of the nook to get breakfast himself.

"Well, if you guys are going to work today, maybe I can grab my stuff from my old apartment with Mark, then possibly get lunch with Slim." I pose the suggestion in a questioning way. We never discussed any rules with me coming back here.

"Sure, if that is what you want to do today. Just make sure Mark is with you at all times," Nico responds quickly and my heart swells. This is what I wanted. My freedom, but with the men I love to share it with. "But Chelsey, please be back no later than four. Dr. Cater is coming for your birth control," he finishes with eyes on me, gauging my reaction.

I nod and drop my eyes as fear swirls in my belly. Marco walks over to me, abandoning his plate. "One of us will be with you, Little Bird. We got you," he says softly before kissing my forehead gently.

"Cool, breakfast is done." Enzo comes striding in the kitchen, shirtless, in a pair of gray sweatpants, his hair still wet from the shower. Normally, I would want to jump his bones, but knowing that my evening will include a visit with Dr. Carter and a birth control shot, has me feeling nauseous.

Enzo's eyes meet mine and his eyebrows pinch together, concern filling his gaze. "What did I miss?"

"We were talking about the day's activities and Dr. Carter is scheduled to come this evening for Chelsey's birth control," Marco informs him.

"Oh. Well if you want us all there with you, we will be." He walks over and kisses me softly.

"Thanks guys. Can we just talk about something else?" I stand to start making my plate.

"Sure thing." Marco smiles. "So, where do you like to go for lunch with your friend?"

Recalling the small little coffee shop downtown, helps to return my smile.

"There's this little place over on Parkway called Jasmines Latte Spot. It's small, but has the best grilled cheese and soup you will ever have. Plus their lattes and house made lemonade is to die for!"

"Well, we won't be able to join you today, but maybe later this week or next you can take us there?" Nic asks before taking another bite of his pancake.

"Absolutely! I love any excuse to go back there!"

"Sounds like a date," Enzo chimes in with a loving smile.

The rest of breakfast is filled with small talk about work, trouble with the drug dealers, and to lighten the mood Marco had to suggest strip poker this evening after the good doctor leaves. I promised to kick all their ass's and I fully intend to keep it. They'll all be naked with hard-ons for me, just begging for me to have my way with them.

Getting dressed for the day, I choose something sensible for packing and moving boxes. It's not much, but still.

Striding into the kitchen Enzo is talking to Mark. I haven't seen the man since I ran away from him. I didn't think about how awkward this might be.

"Hey Mark!" I say cheerfully. It's only awkward if I make it awkward right.

"Miss Ryan, it's good to see you again." He smiles at me. "You look ready to move some boxes. No running this time right," he jokes. That must be a good sign right?

"You have my word, Mark." I smile at him while placing a hand on my heart.

"Alright, I have to get to work and so do you. I'll see you soon, Sweet Peach," Zo says as he cups my chin then kisses me softly. Oh how easy it would be to melt into him and get naked right now.

He pulls away, releasing me. "I love you."

"I love you too."

He leaves me and Mark at the elevator, as he disappears out of the kitchen.

"Are you ready to go?" Mark asks.

"Yes, let's get to work," I say and the elevator pings open.

It feels weird to be leaving the apartment, but this time I get to come back and there is the promise of strip poker tonight.

Chapter 29
Marco

She will be back this evening and she is with Mark so there is no need to worry. But there is this anxiety sitting in my gut that I can't get rid of. She should be out having lunch with Slim by now, but I still find myself checking my phone every five seconds. I'm nowhere near close enough to her if something happens.

Mitch and I are in the southside of Seattle, waiting for Reggie to show up again. And he's always at least an hour late. If he wasn't so damn loyal about feeding us intel, I would put a bullet in his foot to teach him a lesson.

"What do you think he's got this time?" Mitch asks. He always accompanies me, so he knows all the dirty details.

"I'm sure it's the usual, some low life trying to use girls or children as drug runners and we got to put a stop to it. Or maybe someone is picking on the grandmas again," I chuckle. We take every offense seriously, but Reggie likes to act like every little thing is an emergency and we need to call in the whole damn calvary.

"Yeah you're probably right." Mitch shakes his head with a chuckle. "So, I saw that Miss Ryan is back. How is that going?" He raises his eyebrows at me curiously. Mitch knows better than anyone how many ladies I have been with from the club.

"She is fucking perfect man. She is the last girl I will be bring home," I say in all seriousness.

"Wow." He raises his eyebrows at me in shock at the confession. "I'm happy for you guys. Who knew I would see the day where Marco Romano settled down," he teases me and I slug him in the arm while we laugh.

"Look who finally made it," I grumble, my good mood soiled as Reggie makes his way out of an alley and walks toward my car over an hour and a half late. I swear one of these days I'm going to kill this fucking kid.

Mitch and I get out of the car and lean on the hood as Reggie gets close, looking all around for onlookers.

I kind of respect Reggie for the risks he takes for us and his neighborhood. No one likes a snitch.

"This better not be a waste of my time Reggie," I bark at him with a commanding voice. "You kept me waiting again." I steel my voice.

"I know Marco, I'm sorry. But I got something you need to hear." His voice is anxious, and he's still looking around, not making much eye contact. Reggie is always a little paranoid, but never this bad.

My phone pings in my back pocket, and my heart lurches to my throat. *If she needed me, she would call. My Little Bird is okay.*

"Spit it out Reggie, I don't have all day," I command as my phone burns a hole in my pocket.

"Sorry man. So I got a call this morning from David Ryan. He said he couldn't find any new leads down in Cali. Said he is coming back to Seattle and wants to meet in three days."

Fuck. He's coming back here. It's good we got the warning, but apparently our lunch plans are going to have to be put on hold until he is dealt with.

"Thank you. That's good intel. We will be in touch soon," I say with praise and hand him five hundred dollars. Snitches get stitches, but they also get well paid.

"Thanks Marco. Pleasure doing business." He nods at me and smiles then heads for the alleyway he came from.

Immediately, I get back into the car and pull out my phone.

New Message From Ass-Hat Brother

Nic's contact name always makes me smile.

Just as I am pulling up the text, Mitch's phone rings. "Yes, boss?"

"Shit! Okay we are on our way now." He hangs up and throws the car into drive and takes off down the road.

> Ass-Hat Brother: Trouble at Jasmines. Mark is shot. No word from Chelsey. Meet me there NOW!

Chapter 30
Nico

Fucking Seattle traffic never moves fast enough! Damn it, my girl needs me. Move out of the fucking way people!

Finally, I make it to the little coffee shop and Mark is being wheeled into the back of an ambulance.

"What happened? He is the head of my security and guarding my wife." It comes out before I even realize that I just referred to Chelsey as my wife. She isn't, but I don't need any run around from these people right now.

"He has been shot in the abdomen and has passed out from blood loss. We will do everything we can," The EMT reassures me.

My woman is gone, my head of security may die, and Riccardo Altavilla is responsible. Rage boils inside me.

Marco and Enzo show up almost at the same time and rush towards me. Both have fear in their eyes, anger in their firm stances, and determination in their jaws.

"What the hell happened?" Marco says, acid dripping from his tone.

"Riccardo's men took Chelsey and Slim, then shot Mark. He may not make it," I say as calmly as I can manage.

"I am going to fucking kill them," Marco growls and moves to the car.

Enzo grabs him. "We need a plan, but we will get her back and they will pay for this." His firm voice commands, barley keeping a lid on his own anger.

"That's right, even if I have to challenge Riccardo's reign to do it." I growl and they both nod in agreement.

We will burn this world down to find her. We will kill anyone who touches her.

No one takes what belongs to the Romanos.

Acknowledgements

I can't believe it's actually here! This book has been a huge labor of love and at one point I thought it would never be published. Writing this book, gave life back to my bones in a time where I wasn't sure what tomorrow held. So, thank you to you, my lovely readers. Without you, my book with be nothing more than words on a page. I hope this story has brought you joy, and for those who struggle with mental health I hope it makes you feel seen.

This book would not have been published without my amazing support team. Thank you Mom and Grandma for always being the cheerleaders, sounding board, and babysitter so I could disappear to the writing caves. Your support means more than I can express. Etta, thank you for walking along side me no matter what the messages were about. Lastly, Morgan, your expertise and joy in the editing processes was invaluable.

I appreciate all of you so much and thank you for helping my dreams come true.

About The
Author

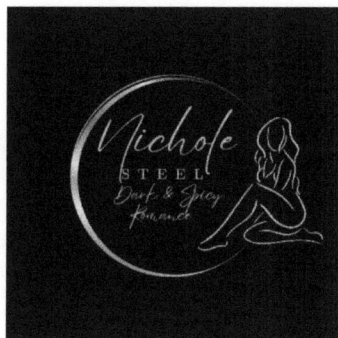

Nichole Steel is a spicy romance author from West Michigan, who is a book worm turned Author. She enjoys writing any thing romance but especially loves creating morally gray characters who are obsessed with their women.

Her other works include Cupid's Crooked Arrow, published with Nicole Frail Books.

Outside of writing she spend her time with her family of six and going on fun adventures in nature.

Find Nichole On:

Instagram: @NicholeSteel.Author

TikTok: @Author.Nichole.Steel

Web: https://bio.site/NicholeSteel

Also by Nichole Steel

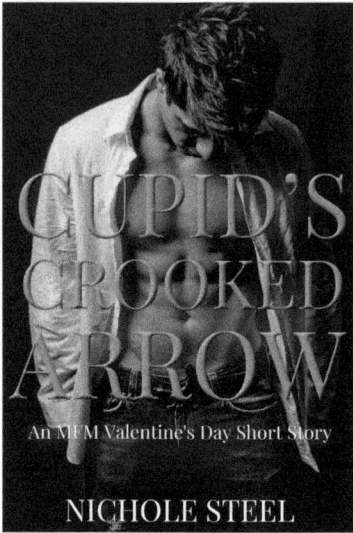

CUPID'S CROOKED ARROW

An MFM Valentine's Day Short Story

NICHOLE STEEL

www.ingramcontent.com/pod-product-compliance
Ingram Content Group UK Ltd.
Pitfield, Milton Keynes, MK11 3LW, UK
UKHW041113110325
455992UK00004BA/238